GOD'S GIFT

Matt O'Donovan

*For those content in uncertainty, able to consider
the other side*

*For those flogged in the street, for questioning if a
man can part the tide*

*For those paralysed by anger, for the injustices
outside*

*For those lashing the whip, whose
humanity has died*

CHAPTER 1

He gripped his head, hunched over on a wooden dining chair. His teeth gritted as he wrestled internally with the voices. Doubt was setting in.

"Don't worry Gary, you've got this!" encouraged God.

"I don't know if I can, this is wrong, this is murder," replied Gary.

"Look, Gary, you've come this far. I mean, you're in her house, aren't you? You've already tied her to the chair, she's already terrified. If you let her go now, not only will you be up 'shit creek' for leaving a witness, you'll also be failing your mission. Your *holy mission!*" God explained.

"I don't want to hurt anyone…" Gary whimpered.

God sighed.

"Gary, you're not going to 'hurt anyone.' You made

the concoction to my instructions, right? *Yeesss*. You sampled it on yourself as I instructed, didn't you? *Yeesss*. And how was it?"

"It was... beautiful," Gary admitted.

"Thank you!" remarked God, triumphantly.

"But I don't understand, why don't you get her to do it?"

"Come on, Gary, you know the rules, if she does it herself then she goes to Hell, and trust me, nobody wants that."

"OK, some other way then, why me, why like this?"

"Mate, what are you talking about? I could give her cancer if you want, you want that? Have her slowly die in agony over years as her family hope, mourn and forget her throughout her weeping life? How about having her crushed to death in a car accident, or have a virus eat her brain on a jungle holiday? You want that, you want that for her? I could, you know."

"Of course I don't."

"Exactly, think of it like this, you're not killing her, you're *saving* her. Fast tracking her to the Gates of Heaven on a cloud of euphoric bliss, painless and free of charge."

"OK..."

Gary removed his hands from his head, sat up straight and looked across the room at her.

She sat still; her mouth gagged with the same brand

of tape that had her fixed to the lounge chair. A small cut on her forehead was dribbling blood over her left eye. She trembled as his gaze met hers.

"It's alright, Mrs McBride, it's alright," Gary said, trying to calm her nerves.

"Mmhmmh," replied Julie, trying to speak.

Gary got up from his chair and delicately made his way over to her, putting his palms outwards to show he was unarmed.

"Mmmhmmm!" she flinched.

"I'm going to take out your gag so we can speak, OK?"

"Mmhm…"

"But, if you scream, I'm going to have to hit you again and we don't want that, do we?" Gary reasoned.

"Mhhm," she nodded.

He reached forward and gently pulled the gag of tape down to her chin, then, with some care, removed the knotted pair of socks from out of her mouth.

She breathed in and out heavily and flexed her jaw.

"Father why are you doing this to me, have I sinned?" a tear mixed with blood ran down her cheek.

"No, of course not, you haven't sinned, quite the opposite in fact. That's why you've been chosen. You've been faithful your whole life."

"I don't understand, who has chosen me, for what?"

"God has chosen you. This is God's gift to you."

"What is God's gift?"

"A pleasurable death."

"Oh god, oh god!" she wept in terror, "You're insane!"

"Listen, God knows about you. He's been watching you. He knows that in 1982, you thought about shaking your baby. It was 4:17 am on a Tuesday night. Your infant was 34 days old and was screaming in his cot, he'd been screaming for 34 days…

"The father of the child, your husband was away on tour, leaving you to deal with Kieran alone. You were sleep deprived and frustrated the baby wasn't bonding with you. You held little Kieran in your arms, you cooed and petted, and offered to feed. But he wouldn't take.

"The room was filled with the gnawing siren of the baby's torment. And, for a fleeting moment, alone and tired, a coldness fell over you; a desire for relief from the living hell you'd found yourself in. For a brief second, frustration nearly overcame you, and the thought of silence, just a moment's silence, became a prize you would kill for…

"You held Kieran out in front of you, screaming at the top of his lungs, and the compulsion to start shaking him began to take over. But as you looked into his eyes you made a choice, you would give your life for his, even if that meant enduring misery. You chose God's selfless love."

Julie McBride looked at Gary slacked jawed.

"How could you possibly know that?"

"God loves you, he truly does, that is why he sent me. You're going to Heaven," Gary smiled.

"Wh... what's it like, Heaven?"

"It's a place where you are truly free, free to indulge in all the urges and fantasies that you have for a lifetime repressed. You will be accepted for the true spirit that you are."

"Will it hurt?"

"What, death? No, well there is a slight pinprick, but what follows is bliss."

Gary reached into his pocket and retrieved a syringe in a sanitation bag.

"How do you know it won't hurt?"

Gary smiled, "God taught me how to make it, it's his recipe."

He removed the syringe, which was three quarters full of a dull golden substance, from the sanitation bag, flicked the needle with his finger then pressed the plunger just enough to remove any air bubbles. He then wrested his hand on her right forearm and tapped for a vein.

"Are you ready?" Gary said calmly.

"No, no, no! I don't want to die!" she cried.

He lifted the needle to her vein and began to pierce the skin.

"Julie, this is God's will, his gift."

"No! Get off me you fucking psycho! No!" she screamed, struggling against her gaffer-tape restraints.

He shoved his spare hand to her mouth, cramming in the bundle of socks.

"Mhmmhmm!"

"Mrs McBride, this is God's gift, you don't have a choice, now relax!" he pushed the plunger, injecting the substance into her veins.

Her eyes lit up.

He removed the socks from her mouth, and she gasped.

Her body began to convulse as the drug took effect.

She gripped his wrist with her hand and clenched uncontrollably. She shook and struggled against the deadly euphoria until finally she became passive… and smiled.

"Thank you, Father," she whispered.

Gary watched and waited as her breathing slowed to a calm and eventual stop.

He stood up, looked down at the corpse and then around the room. It was done.

"Good job, Gary!" God applauded, "now, let's clean up shop, get out of dodge, and then, on to the next one!"

"OK…" Gary thought, working through how to dispose of any incriminating evidence.

"You better get to work, Gary. You haven't got long," God warned.

SOMEWHERE IN HEAVEN

Julie McBride lay on her bed, staring with tired eyes at the dark engulf of the bedroom ceiling. She turned her head to the empty space next to her where her partner once slept, and then to the alarm clock on the bedside table. 4:15 am.

"Please...please...please shut up," she whispered.

Kieran was screaming again.

"OK, OK..."

Julie pulled off the covers, sat up and slumped her feet into her slippers.

"OK, I'm coming, god's sake, Kieran."

She stood up, turned on the light and walked over to his cot.

His distress call was shrill, coarse and deafening like a construction workers hammer drill, biting into a wall.

"What's wrong honey?" she said picking him up carefully.

"What's wrong, huh? You want me to change your nappy?"

She checked his nappy, it was clean.

"No? OK, you hungry? Let's see if you're hungry."

She offered him a feed, but he didn't take.

"Not hungry then, OK, OK?"

The screaming continued; power-tools tearing into brutalist concrete.

"OK, Kier, what do you want?"

She continued to pet him. Her exhaustion and frustration were beginning to peak, and she was getting increasingly anxious about the noise bleeding through the walls and inconveniencing the neighbours, again.

"Kier, Kier, Kier, shush now, come on shush now, shush you little shit."

The baby's screaming intensified, pummelling her eardrums.

"Do you hate me, is that it, do you hate me Kieran?" she shouted, holding the baby in front of her.

"Why do you fucking hate me!?" she sobbed.

"Please just shut the fuck up! Shut up! Shut up! Shut up!"

Tears rolled down her face, and tears turned to anger. 34 days she'd dealt with this. 34 days of no sleep, alone, poor, and depressed.

She looked Kieran in the face, saw his anguished expression, felt her own anguish boil over.

"For fuck's sake! Shut up! Shut up you little fucking demon!" she screamed, as she began to shake, and shake, and shake…

…and

…finally

…there

…was

...silence.

CHAPTER 2

Detective Stephen Mackerel was spinning around on his office chair. Legs lifted off the ground, he watched as the office walls paced past his eyes. He planted his feet at the end of the third rotation, neatly arriving centre desk, with his coffee mug perfectly parallel to his right hand. He picked up the coffee and took a victorious sip, satisfied the new chair was indeed a savvy and enviable purchase. There was a double knock on his window as a head poked through the open door, it was Detective Bracket.

"Hey, Macker. Call just came in, fresh 'rotter' been found 'bout 20k outta town. Wanna take a peek?"

"Sounds like my kinda barbecue," grinned Mackerel in a mock Texan accent, with extra gravel.

"Good man, I'll stick your name on the file," confirmed Bracket.

"Excellent. Also, check it out, huh? Watcha think?" Mackerel said standing up, enthusiastically gesturing to his new chair.

"Oooohh, very nice. Comfy," Bracket remarked as she plonked herself into the seat and started to spin.

"How much you reckon it cost me?" quizzed Mackerel, hoping Bracket would grossly overvalue the product.

"Phhhh, uh dunno, £32.50?" guessed Bracket.

"£28 quid!" Mackerel triumphed, embracing a hefty dopamine reward.

"Not bad. How much was postage and packaging?"

"£20 pounds..." confessed Mackerel, with some frustration.

"Wow, so practically £50 total. That's quite expensive for a 'second hander,' Macker."

"Don't ruin this for me, Bracket!" Mackerel warned with a serious tone, trying to salvage the remains of his short lived and diminishing high.

"OK. It's very nice, well done you," Bracket said with an extra dose of patronisation as she lifted herself up from the second hand 'bargain' and headed for the door.

"Yeah, yeah..." Mackerel nodded sarcastically, then remembered something actually work related, "ah! before you go, who are the available bronze stars with experience in crime scene management? I wouldn't mind touching base with them before I get there... just in case I require them later," asked Mackerel.

"Look at you, going all by the book. Give forensics a call and ask for DCI Emma Fowley, she's pretty good."

Thirty minutes later Mackerel pulled up to the address from the case file. It was a quiet little two story detached house in a quiet little town. The only thing to disrupt the aura of a seemingly tranquil existence was the ambulance and police car parked on the street; that and the thrash metal riffing out of his car stereo, which, even though played at a modest volume, polluted the outside world with growling basslines.

Mackerel, nodding to the rhythm, waited the few extra seconds for the song to finish before he turned off the engine and stepped out of the car. The door shut with a cushioned thud that pleased him. He stole a look at his police issued unmarked car, a metallic black Audi S3. He had been given the choice of a BMW or the Audi, and whilst standing in the mid-afternoon sun, surrounded by the picturesque scenery, he was satisfied that on looks alone the Audi was indeed a savvy and enviable purchase.

Still muttering thrash lyrics, Mackerel became conscious he might get caught gawping at his own car, so quickly snapped back into work-mode. He turned his attention to the scene, surveying the street, getting a feel for the number of houses on the road, the number of parked cars and access routes to and from the house. It hadn't yet been determined if the subject's death was suspicious or not, but as the adage goes: If in doubt, think murder.

Mackerel approached the guard at the door and showed his badge.

"Detective Inspector Mackerel, I'm here about the body."

The guard examined the badge. Satisfied, he handed it back, gave him a nod and opened the door, "come on in sir, they're in the living room, ground floor on the left as you enter."

"Thank you, officer," said Mackerel, stepping through the door.

Mackerel had time to pause again, tuning into the vibe and layout of the hallway, noticing pictures and decorations, colours of walls, carpets and general cleanliness. He squeezed his hands into a pair of disposable blue rubber gloves, took a deep breath and walked into the main room. There, a peaceful looking middle-aged woman sat comfortably on a lounge chair by the front window. Bone still, eyes closed and wearing a faint smile. The first responder paramedic and police officer hovered a few feet away from the body and acknowledged Mackerel's arrival.

Mackerel conducted a brief introduction and then cut to the chase, gathering facts about the case.

"So, what's the story...?" Mackerel asked, now fighting the compulsion to end the sentence with "morning glory?" which, if taken out of context, could be a serious faux pas to make in the presence of professional strangers and a fresh corpse.

"Deceased female, we're guessing in her early 60's. She has an abrasion above her left eye and a small intravenous puncture wound on her right forearm. Time of death? We're not sure, but we estimate it was some time this morning, based on the lack of bodily decay. Cause of death is unclear," replied the police officer.

"Who is she, who found her?" Mackerel followed up, happy to be out of the faux pas danger zone.

"She's been identified as Mrs Julie McBride. Her house cleaner found her this afternoon and called 999."

"OK, where is the cleaner now, did you take a statement?"

"Yes, she left a statement and we allowed her to go home. We let her know that she may be called in for further questioning, if necessary."

"OK, no problem. Do we know if there's any other occupants living here?"

"Unclear, but it appears she lives alone."

"OK, thank you."

Mackerel took a moment to pause and digest the information whilst scanning the room. This was clearly the main living room, which had an open plan kitchen and dining table stretching up to the lounge, where the body rested peacefully.

Something instantly felt amiss, a chink in logic that stood out to Mackerel like a horse with a hump on its back.

"It's very clean and tidy in here isn't it, like, really tidy. Not just this room but the hallway too. Are you telling me that the cleaner turned up, found the body, and then did the housework anyway?" he quizzed the officer.

"According to her statement, no. She turned up at the scheduled time of 1:00pm, found the body, who she recognised as her client Mrs McBride, checked for signs of life, called an ambulance and waited for our arrival," confirmed the officer.

"I see, so, the cleaner didn't clean. OK... let's say the deceased *did*, before she died. Why go to the effort when you know the cleaner is arriving the same day? I mean, this is so fresh I can still smell the chemicals. I suppose one possibility is that she had an onset of dementia, which led to her forgetting about the appointment; an illness that later killed her. A pathologist could confirm that. However, an alternative possibility could be that there was another party here at the time of her death, and this 'other party' then cleaned up the house and bleached the place to cover something up…"

Mackerel felt the former hypothesis was plausible considering his limited knowledge of the deceased, yet he also knew that wiping a scene was a tactic used by organised criminals to destroy forensic evidence.

He went over to inspect the body, crouching over and watching his foot placements, making sure to not disturb the scene as best he could.

The cut above her eye seemed odd and out of context. It was shallow and linear on the brow, like the laceration a boxer suffers when they catch a gloved punch from a bad angle, and not like that of a fall or knock against a solid object, where cuts to the head are usually shorter and deeper.

"Looks like she's been punched," said Mackerel, "either that or she fell and banged her head, but the wound doesn't suggest it."

He stood back up and put his hands on his hips, pondering his available moves. "OK, we have a few options we need to rule out here. It looks like, and most probably is, an accidental or natural death. But the abrasion on the forehead and 'cleaned scene' seems out of place. So, because of these unknown factors, I'm marking this death as suspicious and opening a murder inquiry. This way, we get full access to the resources we need to investigate further. You two will need to stick around and give statements and DNA, hope you haven't got any important plans."

Mackerel stepped outside and dialled the last number on his mobile, "hi Emma, it's DI Mackerel, we spoke a bit earlier. I'm going to need you and your team down here right away."

SOMEWHERE
IN HEAVEN

Jesus picked at the scars on his wrist and flinched with a nervous smile.

"Congratulations, welcome to Heaven," he said, greeting the individuals waiting in line for his autograph.

He was on 'PR duty,' welcoming in new souls. Welcoming the descendants of monsters. Monsters he was sacrificed to save.

He remembered every lash of the whip, every thorn, every nail. His wrists and ankles still ached with the phantom pain. He re-lived the terrifying moments of his crucifixion through nightly flashbacks, waking in cold sweat, screaming for help.

"Congratulations, welcome to Heaven," Jesus

loathed.

He pulled out a chainsaw and revved the engine until the motor growled into life.

"Congratulations! Welcome. To. Heaven!" Jesus snarled as he swung the chomping blade down onto a bemused fan, cutting them in half.

Blood and meat splattered Jesus's face as steel teeth chewed flesh and bone. His pain subsided.

"More," he thought to himself, as he looked upon his obedient cattle.

"More!" he shouted, as he began to work his bloody way through the line.

Julie McBride found herself standing in the queue for Jesus's autograph when she heard a commotion coming from further up the line.

She pushed her way through the forming crowd to get a better look, and to her amazement saw beautiful clouds of crimson vapor, followed by a symphony of screams and howling motors. She was giddy with excitement.

A gap in the crowd appeared and she caught a glimpse of him, Jesus, our savior, white robes drenched in blood, eyes bulging with psychotic intent, waving a chainsaw into all who stood in his way, turning them into twitching, torn, meat giblets.

"Me! Do me next!" Julie heard herself shout.

She felt herself climbing through the masses to get to the bloody center.

"No, do me, do me!" shouted the man next to her.

"No, me!" said another.

Before she knew it, Julie was caught up in a surge of bodies all scrambling to the center of the blender. All eager to acquire the Lord's grotesque signature, the holy kiss of hot steel teeth on flesh.

CHAPTER 3

Mackerel watched passively as a tiny green bird, wearing a bright yellow mohawk, perched on the recently erected police lines which divided the road, cordoning off the scene where Julie McBride's body was found.

"Nature doesn't care for our suffering or triumphs. It just looks on with bemused curiosity..." Mackerel thought to himself as he looked towards the house, to DCI Fowley's troops toing and froing from the house; dressed to the hilt in SOCO suits.

"Nice hairdo, mate. Enjoying the show?" he asked, turning back to the bird. But it was gone, flown away, leaving only the empty police ribbon, swinging gently in the breeze.

"Obviously not then," he assumed. He briefly lifted his eyes to the sky, hoping to spot the Goldcrest, then after a few seconds gave a small sigh, "OK, back to work Macker."

He opened his notepad and walked himself through the murder checklist:

- **Established identity of victim:** Check
- **Secure the scene:** Check
- **Appoint a crime scene manager:** Check
- **Commence the forensic evidence gathering process:** Check
- **Identify possible witnesses:** incomplete – apart from the cleaner who found her.
- **Identify possible suspects:** incomplete – apart from the cleaner who found her.
- **Identify next of kin:** incomplete.
- **Identify a motive:** incomplete.
- **Determine cause of death:** incomplete – possible head trauma – need to wait for the pathologist report.
- **Determine time of death:** incomplete - need to wait for the pathologist report.

"Lots of work to do," he thought as he took out his phone and dialed Bracket's number.

"Hi Macker!" Bracket answered with her typical chirpiness.

"Hi Brum, how's it going?"

"Well, the incident room is being set up as we speak... finding 'next of kin' is in progress... and... we've found out Julie's work address. So pretty good.

How's it going with you?"

"Ah, that is good progress. Yeah, I'm not bad at this end. Fowley's got her team up and running, they're going through the place with a fine-tooth comb as we speak, so if there is any evidence, she'll find it."

"Nice, yep she's a pro. When you heading back?"

"Pretty soon. I'm going to knock a few doors while I'm here, see if anyone's in."

"Good plan, anything else?"

"Nope, just give me a call if anything comes up."

"Will do. See you in a bit!"

"Yep, bye."

Mackerel dipped under the police tape and left the scene, walking up the road to the next property. All the houses were either detached or bungalows. This was a quiet part of suburbia, occupied by well-off city commuters with young families looking for a safe space to nurture life, or retired couples who'd sold up and downsized, intending to live out their golden years in peace then pass away.

It was approaching 3:30pm, so he didn't expect many people to be in as it was still office hours and prime time for school runs. It was also a nice afternoon, so any resident oldies could be out for a walk.

As he suspected, the first few houses drew a blank, but he persevered and stumbled up to a bungalow with a 'noughties era' white ford fiesta parked in the driveway.

"Worth a shot" he thought, looking at his watch. He should really be getting back to the precinct to check in with operations, but he could spare a few more minutes whilst he was in the area.

He pressed the doorbell and waited. About 20 seconds passed with no response.

"Last chance," he muttered to himself as he pressed the doorbell again. This time it was met by a rattling sound followed by some metallic clacking noises as someone fumbled with the lock.

"Hello...?" came a polite but fragile voice from behind the door, as it slowly opened.

A few seconds later, peaking around the gap of the door, appeared an elderly man, hunched over a four wheeled mobility Rollator.

Mackerel knew this was a shaky win. On the one hand he had found a potential witness, on the same street and on the same day as the 'murder.' But, on the other hand, this 'potential witness' looked about 120 years old, and was probably deaf, blind and senile. A tactful and patient approach was needed.

"Hello, sir. My name is Detective Stephen Mackerel. There was an incident down the road this morning, so I'm just going 'door-to-door,' to see if anyone has any information that might help our enquiry..."

"Oh dear," said the old man with worry and empathy.

"If you have five minutes, can I ask you a few questions?" asked Mackerel gently.

"Yes of course. Well, I hope I have five minutes, you never know at my age. I'm very old you see," the old man replied with a dry wit, as a sentient grin lifted his face from the grave.

"Thank you kindly," said Mackerel. He appreciated the humor and felt reassured that not only could the old timer hear him, but he might also not be batshit crazy either.

"Do come in," the old man said as he turned away from the door and began to shuffle down the hall, leading a wobbly path into the house.

Mackerel flicked a glance at his watch and stepped inside. The bungalow was small but perfectly formed, with mobility rails retrofitted to the walls. He followed slowly behind the old man as they made their way to the living room.

It took a good minute to walk the few feet from the front door to the lounge and now the detective watched patiently as the old man carefully maneuvered himself and his Rollator in front of the armchair, which faced a small flat screen TV in the corner. Then, in what seemed like a carefully rehearsed procedure, the old man commenced a very wobbly, very slow attempt to sit down. Mackerel felt himself tense up with anxiety at the spectacle; should he offer help and risk patronising the old fellow or hold back and hope he doesn't fall and break a hip?

Before Mackerel could make a decision, the old man finally let go of the Rollator, fell backwards and thudded into the cushions.

"Mission accomplished," he grinned at the detective.

Mackerel, relieved he didn't have to call an ambulance, nor risk a social faux pas, smiled back and sat down in the chair next to the old man, flipping open his note pad.

"Fire away detective."

"Thank you, sir. Let's start with some easy ones. What is your name?"

"Alan Percy Miller."

"Thank you. Do you mind if I call you Alan?

"That's quite alright detective"

"OK, Alan, how long have you lived at this address?"

"Oh, about 25 years…"

"How old are you, Alan?" Mackerel was asking these formal questions now so that the team could later verify the quality of the evidence and witness statements gathered.

"'I'm 93 years old, my dear."

"Bloody hell, 93!" Mackerel thought, "do you live here alone?" he followed up, not wanting to dwell on his amazement that one could get so old and remain coherent.

"Yes, but I have a carer who visits me."

"OK, thank you, Alan. Do you know a woman called Julie McBride? She lives down the road," Mackerel asked, feeling confident he could move on to questions about the case.

"Julie, yes of course. We're members of the same church. Julie helped me when my wife passed away. She's very good at that. I think she found a fellow lonely spirit in me."

"Did she seem lonely?" Mackerel asked curiously.

"Well, Julie and her husband divorced years ago. He was a nice man, but since his accident he was very troubled, and well, I think that affected the marriage. Their son joined the army like his father, so he's out of country a lot."

"What happened to the husband to make him troubled?" Mackerel probed after making a note. He knew that troubled husbands could often lead to dead wives.

"Sean, he was hurt in combat. He got what we call 'shell shock'..." Alan paused, thinking about the line of questioning the detective was pursuing, "Tell me detective, is Julie in trouble?"

"Alan, I'm so sorry, but I'm afraid Julie died, sometime in the last 24 hours."

"Oh dear." The man was genuinely moved with emotion. He stared into the distance with a sad contemplation in his eyes, "what happened to her?"

"We're not sure at the moment. We're just trying to

find out if anyone has seen or heard *anything* that may help us. For example, has Julie left the house or had any visitors in the last 48 hours? Have you seen anyone or anything down the street that felt out of place or unusual, or any people who don't live on the road, or her ex-husband Sean, for example?"

"No, I don't think so… well, apart from Gary this morning…"

"Gary?" Mackerel scribbled this new name in his pad.

"Yes, he's one of our local vicars. They often visit the area, knocking on doors, checking in on us oldies."

"What time was this, did Gary visit you this morning as well?"

"Oh, I'm not sure of the exact time, but it must have been around brunch, as I was in the kitchen. No, he didn't visit me…but I saw him out my kitchen window. He seemed in a hurry; I think he was talking to someone."

"What direction was he going, in relation to Julie's house?"

"He was going up the road. So, away from Julie's."

Mackerel, knowing this was an actual lead, took more notes and flipped to a new leaf in his pad, "what can you tell me about Gary?"

"Oh, he's a lovely young man, very faithful. An honest and kind gentleman."

"How old is he, what does he look like?"

"Oh, late 30's early 40's. But it's hard to tell at my age. What does he look like? Average height, a bit skinny, brown hair, fare skin."

"Thank you very much, Alan."

Mackerel thought for a moment and flicked though his notes. "You mentioned you thought he was talking to someone. Why would you think that, was somebody else with him?"

"No, he was alone, from what I saw...but he was gesticulating with his hands like he was talking..."

"Was he on the phone, perhaps?"

"I don't know I'm afraid, I can't remember," the old man was getting tired.

Mackerel supposed the vicar could have been on hands free, and wondered who he could have been talking to, the church or a spouse perhaps?

"What was his demeanor, did he seem happy, angry, sad?"

"I... can't remember. I'm very sorry..." Alan said, trying his best.

"OK, thank you for your time today, Alan. You have been *extremely* helpful," Mackerel could see the old man was getting exhausted by the questions and thought it was best to wrap up.

"Oh, that's OK detective, if you just wait a minute, I'll see you to the door," Alan said reaching for the Rollator.

"Don't worry, Mr Miller. I can see myself out," Mackerel replied, thinking it probably safer, and definitely more time efficient to decline Alans offer, "can I get you anything before I go?"

"A glass of orange squash would be lovely, if you don't mind."

Mackerel got the man his drink, said his goodbyes, then left him to his chair, juice and TV. He walked back through the kitchen to look out the window; it had a clear view of the street, where according to Alan, the vicar had walked past in a hurry, around the possible time of death.

On his way back to the car, he made sure to ask the Crime Scene Manager, DCI Fowley, to extend the scope of the scene beyond the old man's house. If this vicar was the killer, he might have dropped some evidence further up the street.

After confirming the situation with Fowley and happy the scene was in safe hands, he hopped back into his unmarked car, but this time was too preoccupied to acknowledge the car's aesthetic beauty, nor his astute consumer decision making. He turned off the stereo before it could blast guitar riffs at him; he wanted the silence to focus on his thoughts as his mind was buzzing with questions, new information and procedure.

SOMEWHERE
IN HEAVEN

Julie McBride's body twitched with ecstasy. This was bliss. This was Heaven.

She was in the center of writhing bodies, groaning and howling, slipping and sliding over each other like lizards in a pit.

Blood and gore seeped from their wounds. Each soul thrashing over each other, molesting, kissing, biting. Each touch a blast of lava-hot pleasure.

They were one with Jesus. Jesus was one with them. They were one with each other.

Bright lights filled the sky; small stars burning amber against a clear blue sheen.

The shimmering dots grew larger and larger, closer

and closer, until Julie, heaving and grunting in the bloody mass, realised that they were not stars but Angels.

"Oh, my," she thought.

"Oh, my," tears of joy seeped down her face.

First tens, then hundreds of Angels flocked, and with them, on the ground, a rumble and a thunder of pounding feet as scores of souls charged from the corners of Heaven into the mass, climbing, groping, fighting and wounding. Tearing at eyes and mouths, biting and clawing, eating into the pileup, zoning in on Jesus.

With torn robes and wild eyes, Jesus arched his head back and howled like a wolf at the sky of Angels.

He swung his chainsaw over his head like a propeller, spinning himself like a deadly top, carving up the new surge of worshippers like a meat blender.

The Angels descended, glowing golden skin and emerald eyes, wielding an arsenal of medieval clubs, swords, barbed nets, spears and machine guns, unleashing madness and bloodlust on the ever-growing congregation.

The Angels tore and fought, bashing in skulls, lashing backs, piercing bellies, unloading rounds of lead bullets into heaps of undulating bodies.

Screams of pain and anguish filled the air.

Feelings of divine pleasure filled the inner space of each soul.

This was mass. This was congregation.

Julie couldn't believe her luck. Mass with Jesus and a flock of Angels. An indoctrination into Heaven by the lord himself.

Who can say they were touched by an Angel? Who can say they've lain in the presence of the Holy Father?

She turned her head to the soul next to her; a man writhing in a bloody heap. His face contorted with a twisted horror.

Their eyes met. She smiled and he smiled back.

She licked the gaping wound on his face.

It tasted like honey.

She bit into the wound.

He screamed and struggled.

Thrashing he bit back.

She screamed.

Once again, their souls burned with ecstasy.

They started to eat each other.

This was Heaven.

Souls becoming one.

CHAPTER 4

The incident room was modest in size. A large rectangle table took up most of the space. Evidence boxes piled up against the back wall whilst a white board dominated the front wall. Cork boards ran eye height along the side walls, where photos of Julie McBride, both when alive and deceased, along with pictures of the scene were pinned.

Nine detectives sat around the table.

"Hey, Mackerel, get this...I ordered an americano with skinny milk but I'm fairly sure it tastes full fat. What d'ya reckon, should I open a murder investigation?"

Laughter.

"Mack-Mack, my freezer defrosted all over the kitchen floor. Think I'm going to open a murder inquiry."

More laughter.

"Oi, Macaroni cheese, I looked out the window and opened a murder investigation."

Cheering.

"Shots fired, Mackerel's taking bullets," jibed Bracket.

Mackerel raised his voice above the noise and abuse, "OK, OK, as you all know, we've opened a murder investigation into the death of a Mrs. Julie McBri-"

"You mean, *you've* opened a murder investigation," interrupted Detective Dubois.

"Yes, Nigel, I've opened a murder investigation, because the evidence at the scene suggests Mrs McBride's death may have occurred in suspicious circumstances. Thus, the correct protocol is to open a murder inquiry, which you would know if you'd passed your PIP level 3 exam instead of passing pips into your socks...you wanker," Mackerel retorted, rocking his closed fist from side-to-side at Dubois, hoping it would be taken for the banter it was.

Another detective who had remained quiet spoke up, "alright, alright that's enough. We don't have much time, so let's get on with it, shall we? For those who don't know me, I'm Detective Peters, the assigned Program Manager for this murder inquiry which, with ribbing Mackerel aside, has been given added credibility from the initial forensic work of DCI Emma Fowley's team.

"As such, we've been allocated budget and resource

to continue the investigation, for now. But as we should all know, resources do dry up, so time is of the essence. I'm aware that some of you have worked with each other before, and some have been pulled in from various local departments. So, with that in mind, let's all introduce ourselves for the meeting register, then Mackerel will divvy up the roles."

The remaining detectives called out their names.

"I'm DI Stephen Mackerel, lead detective for the investigation," he said, giving two thumbs up.

"DI Birmingham Bracket, reporting for duty, sir!" she said, saluting with a wry smile.

"I'm DI Nigel Dubois," he raised a middle finger to the group.

"Simon Crease, Detective Constable," he flicked a shallow nod.

"DI June Dune," she sat back with arms folded.

"DS Yolanda Spark, here," she said looking at her notes.

"I'm DI Susan Handy," she gave a small wave.

"DCI Emma Fowley. Crime Scene manager," she said formally, observing the group.

"OK, looks like everyone is here, thank you," said Peters, ticking off the names. He then gave Mackerel a nod.

Mackerel refenced his notes and got into his groove, "OK, as you know, we are in the golden twenty-four hours of the investigation, this means witness memories are fresh and evidence is not yet spoiled by time. How we act now will greatly influence our success or failure in solving this case.

"Here's how the teams are divided: Spark and Crease - you're on CCTV, look for any cars and/or people leaving or arriving at the scene within 24 hours of time of death, find a pattern.

"Handy and Dubois – you're interviewing Sean McBride, the ex-husband. He's a key person of interest until he's not.

"Bracket and I - we'll be following up on Gary 'the vicar', who was spotted near the scene this morning. We're treating him as a key person of interest for now.

"Fowley - continue heading up the forensics and DNA side of things.

"Dune - you're evidence manager, so everyone will need to touch base with you.

"Peters - as stated, is program manager and budgets, if anyone needs more resource or wants to log complaints about Dubois, Peters is the guy. All good?"

"Safe bruv!" replied Bracket, with a quasi-urban inflection.

Sue Handy turned to Nigel Dubois and said with a smile, "You wonna be good cop or bad cop?"

An hour later Mackerel and Bracket pulled up to the church in question; a council-built community hall in the form of a two-story concrete slab.

"I don't really get these places," said Mackerel, candidly.

"OK...? What's not to get?" quizzed Bracket, slightly bemused.

"I just feel they're kind of depressing, you know. People worshipping a higher power when there's no tangible evidence that the 'higher power' even exists. People restricting their lives for it, then expecting some kind of farfetched reward in return..."

"That is very cynical Macker. Have you thought that, maybe, church helps people cope with some troubled aspect of their lives, or, that many people just go for the social and community aspect, tea and biscuits and company?" countered Bracket.

"Yeah, or it's a corrupt institution, designed to control people who can't think for themselves?"

"What happened Macaroon, did you get bummed at Sunday School, or something?" she looked at him with a mock understanding smile.

Mackerel laughed, "Whatever, anyway we're not here to pull a Richard Dawkins on these people. Let's see if anyone knows this 'Gary' character."

"You started it."

Mackerel opened the door and walked in with Bracket in tow. The main hall was empty of worshippers. Two lanes of vacant wooden pews faced the small altar, punctuated by purple drapes that wore the church insignia hanging from the back wall. The faint sound of local radio played from deep within the building.

Following the noise, the detectives navigated the tight and winding corridors, using the radio's volume as a guide.

"And that was Lady Booty Mumma with her top 10 smash hit 'Deep-Bounce.' Let us know if you're feeling the booty, call or text 03050 0444 7299101. Next, we have the up-and-coming indie rock sensations The Letter Boxes, with their debut single 'Hope is Fire.'"

"Ooh, I like The Letter Boxes," Bracket whispered to Mackerel.

The song started with a jangly guitar intro, followed by a repetitive one-note bassline, backed by pitter-patter snare drums. The frontman then began to sing, howling like the family cat, just before its sick on the carpet.

'I see your face

When I lose the chase

Hope is in the fireplace…

A heart for hire

A burnt car tire
An electric wire
Hope Is fire!

Yeah!'

"Sounds like Jim Morrison pseudo poetry to me," whispered Mackerel in critique.

"They're catchy. 'Hope is fire… byooing,'" Bracket replied as she whispered along to the lyrics, mimicking the guitar with her voice.

Mackerel snarled.

"What bands do you like then Mr culture snob."

"Uh, well, I have a very eclectic taste, actually. But currently I'm experimenting with various subgenres of punk and heavy metal, things like hardcore, thrashcore and anti-culture rotcore, you know, bands like Anal Discharge, Half-Eaten-Fetus, Bulimic Detonator…'"

"Never heard of them…but they sound shit," whispered Bracket.

"Some of them have surprisingly astute social-political commentary, I'll have you know. For example, Bulimic Detonator has a song called 'Vomit Influencer', their lyrics go:

'You got one hundred thousand followers

So, you think that you matter

One hundred thousand particles
of vomit splatter...'

"Good huh?" whispered Mackerel.

"Sounds angry," observed Bracket.

"Yeah, they're well angry," grinned Mackerel, "they got another one called 'Holy Horse Shit', which goes:

'If God made the world

He shat it out his arse

Control us with your words

Religion is a farce...'

"Yeah, that's probably not appropriate lyrics for the current situation, Macker," whispered Bracket, wondering if the song had influenced Mackerel's current philosophical unease towards theism or vice versa.

"Not appropriate, this place was playing Deep-Bounce by Lady Booty Mumma a few minutes ago, have you heard those lyrics, it's basically audio-porn!" said Mackerel, forgetting to control his volume.

"Shush...you're getting too loud!" Bracket whispered, "and don't slag off the 'Booty Mumma,' she's a-"

"Hello, who's there?" called a voice from one of the back rooms, interrupting their debate. The voice was barely audible over the jangly nonsense of The Letter Boxes.

"Police," shouted Bracket in response.

Bracket and Mackerel followed the voice to a closed door, the music now at modest volume. They hung back for a second, coordinating with each other with hand signals, then entered through, finding themselves in a small kitchen with a middle-aged priest, in full robes, filling up a tray with mini triangle sandwiches.

"Hello sir, I'm Detective Mackerel and this is Detective Bracket," Mackerel said assessing the situation.

"Oh hello," said the priest, turning the radio off, "would you like a cheese sandwich?"

"No thank you, sir," replied Mackerel in a volume awkwardly loud for the now quiet room.

The priest gestured to Bracket, "cheese sandwich?"

"Oh, I'm alright thanks," Bracket smiled, also turning down the offer.

"OK, what can I do for you, detectives?" he asked politely, wrapping the tray of sandwiches with clingfilm.

"We're investigating an incident in the local area" Mackerel said, not revealing his cards straight away, "does a vicar called Gary work here?"

"Oh, yes, Gary Uxbridge, he's been with us a few years now. Nice chap, very dedicated to his faith.

Why?"

"We think Gary may have some information that could aid our inquiry, any chance he's in today?"

"I'm afraid not. In fact, I haven't seen him for a few days, come to think of it..."

"Shouldn't he be checking back in today, after he's finished visiting church members?" asked Bracket, probing strategically.

"He would do normally, yes, but Gary hasn't had any arranged bookings for today."

Bracket and Mackerel exchanged a look; his eyebrows raised, and a sense of urgency framed her expression. She hastily left the room and dialed into HQ, "please update all units, Gary Uxbridge is now a prime suspect, his whereabouts are currently unknown..."

The priest looked stunned.

"What information can you give us on Gary?" Mackerel asked the priest.

"What kind of information do you need?"

"Address, habits, does he have a spouse, anything odd about his behavior?"

"No, well..." the priest stopped and chuckled to himself, "Gary has talked a lot recently about 'speaking with God.'"

"OK, isn't that normal for... you guys?" Mackerel said politely, trying not to appear ignorant.

"To a degree, yes, we pray, and we hope God listens."

"So, how is Gary any different?"

"He says God speaks back."

"So… he's gone crazy…?" said Mackerel tentatively, trying to make sense of the priest's answers without being offensive.

"There is a difference between faith and delusion, detective. Who am I to judge another man's experience of the Holy Spirit, especially that of a fellow clergyman, we are not evangelical here."

"So, you… *don't* think he's delusional?" Mackerel puzzled.

"It is rare for us to claim God has spoken to us directly. But perhaps it is true. Perhaps God does speak to Gary," mused the priest, "I would be unfaithful if I closed my heart to the possibility."

"Fair enough. Let's just say his behavior has been unconventional, of late, right?" Mackerel said, jotting the compromise down in his pad, "do you know where Gary might be? It is extremely important that we find him."

"Well, I assume he's probably resting up at home… Tell me, what do you think he's done, detective?"

"We think he might be involved in the death of one your church members," said Bracket, returning from the labyrinthine corridors.

"I'm sorry, detective, but I find that awfully hard to

believe… Gary is a gentle soul who loves the congregation. He wouldn't hurt anybody."

"Look, we're keeping an open mind, OK… but like you said, he's been acting strange lately and you haven't seen him for a few days. He might be, you know, 'unwell,' so we need to find him. You said he's probably at home, can you give us his address, please?" said Mackerel, diplomatically, whilst offering the priest a pen and a leaf from his note pad.

The priest scribbled Gary's address on the scrap of paper, "here is his house number and street, I can't remember the full details I'm afraid…but he's based in town."

"OK, this will do, for now, we'll run it through our systems to get the rest." Mackerel pocketed the scrap of paper with the address, "thank you for your co-operation today, sir, we'll be in touch."

SOMEWHERE
IN HEAVEN

Jesus walked over the chunks of bloody meat as it festered, rotted and decayed.

He walked though fields of crosses. Acres of them. Each erected in his name. Each with a soul nailed to the wood. Each moaning in agony.

They were participating in a great reenactment, an homage to the holy death, a tribute to the Father who died for their sins.

An empty gesture. They would never know his pain.

Like always, these acts of barbarism failed to give Jesus the kick he needed. Pain in Heaven was merely the façade of pain, the face of it, it was not real.

He needed to go where the pain was real. For then, maybe, he could truly process his own.

He walked towards a collection of trees, away from the moaning fields of sticks. There, he gave an instinctive glance over his shoulder, making sure he'd arrived unseen, then, in the shade, he opened a portal to Hell and stepped inside.

Hidden behind a boulder in the mouth of a tunnel, Jesus peered through a gap in the rock.

For what seemed like hours, he had tracked the noxious smell of burning flesh, and the demented sounds of agonising pain. Now he could finally see it.

A group of souls, four of them. Two male and two female, stuck, fixed like pilons in the center of a small but raging fire pit, observed by a squad of Demons.

Jesus, still peering through the crack watched the Demons move. The similarities to the Angels in Heaven were uncanny, like an alternative interpretation of the same idea.

Their movements were sharp and jarred, not fluid and graceful. Their wings, leathery and torn. Their skin, not golden and glorious, but ash white, broken and cracked by the smoldering embers beneath.

He waited for the Demons to move on to another part of the greater Hell pit, then made his way closer to the burning souls.

As he approached, he could begin to clearly make out the features of the soul burning nearest to him, a male, naked and stuck.

He watched intrigued as the man's skin melted in the fire, then melted again and again, as if it was caught in a time loop.

The four souls were each in a state of constant start and reset, yet their eyes told of a consciousness that never ceased to bear witness to their own suffering.

True pain.

The man's eyes focused on Jesus and began to weep, then they all saw him, and they all wept, sobbing uncontrollably.

"I'm sorry, Father, My Lord, please forgive me, I beg of you," they cried.

True anguish. Real.

"Do not fret my children. I'm busting you outta-here," Jesus whispered.

He then knelt by the edge of the fire pit and prayed.

As he prayed, the fire lost its intensity.

His face was calm, his hands pressed together.

The fire shrank further until it was nothing more than black coal and smoke.

Jesus rose to his feet. The soul's skin no longer melted. The loop was broken.

Hope and joy beset the tormented bodies for the first time this side of eternity.

"Thank you, My Lord. Thank you! You saved me,"

they each said.

"Shush!" Jesus snapped with a warning, "we're not out of this yet, come, this way, follow me!"

"Where are you taking me?" they asked.

"Heaven!"

As a group they ran, Jesus up front and the four scorched, naked bodies in tow.

They followed Jesus's path, through cave tunnels and over bridges of flesh and bone, until they arrived back to where Jesus had left the portal.

"Shit!" Jesus said, looking back at the souls, "it was right here, I'm sure of it."

At that moment, a squad of Demons emerged from the shadowy walls of the tunnel and surrounded them.

"Oh God, oh Jesus, do something, please save me, I can't go back to the pits, I can't!" each of the souls begged in terror.

"Jesssussss...?" a Demon hissed.

It grinned at Jesus with an Angel-like face, heavily scarred, it's lips, nose and eyelids burnt off.

"Ssssaaviorrrr....?"

It then plunged its flaming pitchfork into Jesus's chest, piercing his body and setting his robes ablaze.

The four scorched, naked souls looked on in horror as their savior fell. Their dreams of escape snuffed out.

The Demon turned back to the souls and grinned.

"No sssaaviorr. Taaake them baaack to the fiiire piiitsss."

CHAPTER 5

"This is Radio Best and next up is Lady Booty Mumma with 'Deep Bounce.'

'...Dollar, Dollar, Dollar, Dollar, Dollar, Dollar

Gimmi da, Gimmi da, Gimmi da Dollar

I want it, want it, want it, want it, want it, want it deep

Give ya that deep bounce, booty bounce,

Lady Booty Mumma in da house

Gonna give ya that deep bounce, booty bounce

Cos Lady Booty Mumma in da house

Gimmi da Dollar, Dollar, Dollar, Dollar Dol-'

Scrrrrrchhhhhhh

"I feel stupider for listening to that," Mackerel said as he flicked the radio to white noise.

He checked the Satnav. His car was being represented by a small pixelated blue circle, jerking along a magnolia path, which could have easily been a river or a road. He'd purchased the device refurbished from eBay, saving himself £50 off an equivalent branded model. It performed reasonably enough, but it was too early to tell if it was indeed a savvy and enviable purchase.

'...give ya that deep bounce, booty bounce
Cos Lady Booty Mumma in da hou-'

"Hello, Bracket speaking... yep, great, send over some bobbies...yep, tell them to pack the sledge-hammer... yep, bye!" Bracket said, hanging up the phone.

"You made it your *ring tone*?" Mackerel asked exasperated.

"Lady Booty Mumma in that house..." Bracket sang, pouting her lips and bobbing her head from side to side.

"Postcode?"

"JO7 9XN,"

"Alright, lets slap it in."

Mackerel found a place to pull over.

"Hang on…" he squinted his eyes and pressed the destination button on the re-furbished Satnav. There was no response.

"I think it's crashed," he said with disappointment, the irony not lost on him, "we're gonna have to use your phone."

They pulled up to Gary's address, a narrow three-story town house. The ground floor was fronted by a scabby garage and side entrance door.

Mackerel pressed the bell, there was no answer.

"Well, looks like nobody's home," said Mackerel, after ringing the bell a few more times.

"No surprise there then…" Bracket replied.

"*Lads?*" Mackerel said to the officers behind him.

A six-foot five, squared shouldered thug in a police high-vis jacket, strutted to door.

"*Clear!*" he warned, with a gruff geezer voice.

He clattered a heavy battering ram into the keyhole, crunching the center of the door into an arc, leaving it barely hanging on to its hinges.

"*Clear!*" he smashed the top corner, followed with the bottom and the door flung open in a crumpled heap.

"Good job Josh. Remind me *not* to call you if I lose my keys," Mackerel said, pleased with his cool quip.

They stepped through the demolished entrance and into a dirty corridor. It ran along the outside of the garage and led up some concrete stairs to Gary's actual front door on the first floor.

The officers checked the garage first, then climbed the stairs to the front door.

Mackerel gave it a knock.

"Gary? Gary, can you hear me? This is the police, open up!"

There was no answer.

Mackerel gave the nod.

Josh, the police thug with the battering ram, stepped up, and with two thuds and a crunch, the door swung open.

Two police, armed with tasers, walked inside and swept the area.

"Clear."

"Clear."

Mackerel and Bracket exchanged a glance and nodded.

"Lady Booty Mumma in da house," Bracket mouthed silently, bobbing her head side to side.

The first thing they noticed inside the house was the

smell. It was acidic, like vinegar, mixed with a whiff of damp.

The hall was dark, Mackerel found a light switch and flicked it on, revealing magnolia walls folding into a grey short-wool carpet. A small ornamental cross hung alone on the wall.

"Detectives, you may want to take a look at this," said one of the taser police from deeper in the flat.

Mackerel and Bracket followed the voice to the living room.

"Holy shit!" they exclaimed in unison.

Sprawled out on the grungy dining table was an array of oddly shaped glass jars and tubes, buckets, and gas burners.

"It's a fucking chemistry lab," said Mackerel.

"What do you reckon he's been making?" pondered Bracket.

"Dunno? but it's not a 'Brew-Your-Own-Beer kit,' that's for sure."

Mackerel then turned to Bracket, "the intravenous wound on Julie McBride!"

"So, he's cooked up some gunk and pumped it right into her veins, then the poor old dear overdosed on the stuff?" asked Bracket.

"Yeah, could well be. Maybe she's even a user and he's a cook for some fucked-up holy drug-ring. Fuck, if I knew church was this much of a party, I'd have signed up years ago! Looks like religion really is the opiate of the people," Mackerel riffed, fired up by the new discovery and unleashing awesome new quips.

Bracket rolled her eyes.

"Right, nobody touch nothing!" Mackerel instructed, snapping back into work mode, "this is a new scene. Let's get Fowley and her forensic crew down here ASAP. No one else in or out. I want the place dusted for prints. I want DNA. I want samples of whatever the fuck it is that's been cooked up in this 'junior-school science project,' and I want it cross examined with Julie McBride's blood samples. I bet anyone £50 quid it's a match."

Mackerel grinned at Bracket with excitement. They were hot on the trail.

SOMEWHERE
IN HEAVEN

God sat in it's throne room facing the window overlooking one of many possible courtyards.

This particular courtyard was a luscious orchard, symmetrically divided by a gold tiled path.

Each apple on each branch was perfectly formed for what it was. For all forms that could exist did exist in a perfect representation in Heaven. They shifted in size, colour and shape. The fruit could be decomposed and humming with wasps, or fresh and ripe, or simply budding. They were triangular shaped, square, round, green, purple or black. Whatever they could be they were and simultaneously were not.

God looked upon it's shape shifting orchard, a paint pallet of options for earth.

"What's the numbers?" it asked its assistant.

"Down, Gov.' Negative 2% year on year. They're living longer."

God mused silently to itself on the absurdity.

It turned and faced the assistant. God itself shape shifted like the orchards, taking on the form of every possible idea of a living entity, human, animal, insect. She was Buddha, she was Allah, he had a long grey beard and pale skin, it was a dog, a cat, a stick insect, a mouse with a human ear on its back. All possible forms existing in one entity, flitting between identities. Only those who bear witness to God could define its form, and only then subjectively.

"They're...enhancing their medical technologies, Gov.' They're still trying to postpone death," said the assistant.

"Idiots. Have they forgotten why they are there? Why do they wish to increase their time on the naughty step, don't they want to come home? What is going on?" asked God.

"Well, they find the thought of death quite unpleasant, sir. They fear it," said the assistant.

"But surely they know that in death they come home?"

"Earth cultures are becoming far more secular, Gov.' Organized religion is decreasing. We're just not getting the word out."

"Fucking marketeers. No wonder it's been so hard finding new prophets of death down there."

"In regard to prophets of death, Gov,' how is your new project?"

"So, so. Gary has faith, which is rare, but...well let's just say he's a complete pussy. Getting a believer to *actually believe* is quite a challenge. He's been completely brainwashed, conditioned by their soft-core versions of the scripture. I mean those books were written thousands of years ago and translated by illiterates. Someone needs to re-write an up-to-date hardcore version. None of this wimpy shit. You know what I mean...? But alas, the new concoction works fine, takes the edge off the passing. Better than a train wreck," God winked with its infinite eyes.

"How's the new guest, Gov'?"

"Julie, yep she's settled in fine. She's taken the same 'forbidden pleasure' route that all humans do. But I guess that's what happens when you enforce the repression of biological instincts on an entire species. I mean, I understand that they want to have experiences that were forbidden on earth, free of consequence. I'm happy with that, it wouldn't be much of an afterlife if they couldn't, would it. But Jesus always has to take it too far, riling them up, exploiting their love for him, and to be honest, creating a bloody mess."

"How is your son, any progress?"

"Nope, he's still not speaking to me. Think he's still upset that I abandoned him."

"Well, they did torture him to death, Gov.' Some of the others believe he's showing signs of 'PTSD.' It's not like he gets the slate wiped clean when he's, you know, home. He still suffers from the memory."

"He's being a spoiled brat is what it is...anyway, enough about him. Gary's onto the next one as we speak, a few more tests and we can roll this method out into full production."

"It will be much more targeted than the tsunami approach, at least, Gov."

"Exactly! It allows us to get 'em when they're good without handing over a blanket of bad eggs to Lucifer in the wash up. It's also positive PR with the 'inmates' as it shows we're prepared to reduce sentences based on good behavior, so, a win-win really. Besides, Gary is turning out to be an interesting little project, and we all need a good project… otherwise, what's the point."

"What's the point of...what, Gov?"

"Existence, my friend. Existence."

CHAPTER 6

Gary sat in his car at the roundabout, waiting for a gap to appear.

"Take the third exit," instructed God.

A gap appeared. Gary eased on the gas and released the clutch. The car jerked forward, threatening to stall. He tempered the clutch, found the bite-point and lurched into his lane. He waved a thank you to the Mini Cooper he had now cut up, then, indicating late, he exited off the third exit, cutting up more traffic. He was tired and flustered.

He followed the main road and passed a sign signaling 'Greenbourne, 200 yards.'

"Take the exit for Greenbourne," said God.

Gary did as he was instructed.

"This is it, he's about 5 minutes away."

Gary looked at himself in the reflection of the window, "am I mad, how am I going to get away with this?"

"Gary, me ol' chestnut, don't worry about that. Big daddy's got your back."

Gary had been having doubts since Julie.

"She didn't want to go, she wasn't ready."

"They're never ready to begin with, Gary. It's fear, you see, fear of the unknown, fear that this world is all they have."

"Why did you give us fear?"

"Well, the species wouldn't last long without fear. It's what keeps you alive. But it's what keeps you trapped. The best type of prison is the one the inmates are afraid to leave.

Gary reflected on his activities of the last nine hours since leaving Julie McBride, his first kill.

Those activities were: driving, sleeping in his car, eating at service stations, fretting, questioning his sanity, drinking coffee, waiting for his next instruction.

God wasn't always with him. Sometimes for hours. Sometimes for days he'd be left with only the noise of his own thoughts.

How could he know God wasn't just more noise of the mind? Only faith, and the fact that the signal was clear, pure and direct. Not nebulas shifting chatter. It was objective and abstract from himself, simultaneously foreign and within. Not possession, but conversation.

That conversation started again, fifty minutes ago and now he was approaching his next objective. His second prisoner to set free. He didn't know how many more there were, or when his task would be complete. That was God's mystery.

Gary approached his destination and felt the butterflies flapping around inside his stomach.

He pulled over to the curb a few places down from the objective and checked his dog collar in the rear-view mirror. Happy he looked presentable, he reached a gloved hand into a leather satchel and returned a syringe filled with a golden substance, put it in his inner coat pocket and stepped out of the car.

He was a man wracked with doubt. He was a man glowing with faith. For a man of faith must be a man of doubt. For without doubt there is no requirement for faith.

"Come on Gazza! Send him home!" cheered God with encouragement.

Gary took a deep breath, tugged his coat and stepped forwards to the objective. He pressed the doorbell and waited. He stared at the white, painted door and went into himself. His face sagged as he disconnected from the outside world.

The door unlocked with a couple of click-thuds. Gary snapped out of his daydream. He adopted a smile, a friendly welcome for a face he had never seen before.

A middle-aged man answered the door.

"That's him," said God.

Gary decided to introduce himself, "Hello, my names Gar-"

"I'm sorry, I don't speak to Jehovah's Witnesses," interrupted the man.

"... Oh, but I'm not a Jehovah's Witness, sir, I'm with the-"

"Yeah, I don't take canvassing either, did you not see the sign?" the man interrupted again, flicking his eyes in the direction of the window, where sure enough blared a yellow sign:

'No canvassing, marketing, sales or Jehovah's Witnesses. Thank you!'

The man started to close the door, smiling politely.

"Jonathan!" blurted Gary.

"Sorry, do I know you?" said the man with a be-mused expression.

"No."

"OK, how do you know my name then?"

"My names Gary Uxbridge, I'm with the Church of England," he shuffled his coat open to make his dog collar more visible, "do you mind if I come in?"

"Well, yes I do mind, it's late and my tea's getting cold."

"I have a gift. I've travelled a long way to give it to you."

"A gift? What gift?" said the man with curiosity.

"A reward, for your personal sacrifice."

"My sacrifice?" the man squinted his eyes in confusion.

"Yes, the sacrifice of enduring your burden, your disease, your test."

"What fucking disease?"

"May I come in?"

"No, you may not. Look, I don't mean to be impolite but tell me what you want or fuck off."

Gary wondered why God would ever want to save this intolerant and dissenting man.

God told him why. Gary repeated his words, "You've abstained from your urges, denied your sinful programming."

"I beg your pardon?" Jonathan said, exasperated.

"You've never acted on your compulsion, the compulsion to sleep with children. You have locked yourself away. You sacrificed your needs and desires to save them from that sin. God sees that. God wants to reward you."

"How fucking dare you! Get off my property before I call the police!" he tried to slam the door, but Gary jammed his foot in the way, blocking it from closing.

"What are you doing?" the man said angrily.

Gary said nothing, instead he shoulder-barged the door, knocking back the man, and stormed into the house.

"Hey!?" yelped Jonathan, in a scared, high pitch tone.

Gary, now in the hallway, grabbed Jonathan and shoved him backwards, knocking pictures and ornaments off a vintage wooden cabinet, which was now pressing into the man's lower back.

"Don't you see, God has a gift for you. You are going to Heaven. You are saved!" Gary shouted through his gritted teeth.

"Get off me! Karen!"

Leaning his weight against the man, Gary reached into his inner pocket. Fumbling, he pulled out the syringe and flicked off the plastic cork covering the needle point.

"Oh my god! Karen, help!"

Gary shifted his weight and with his full force attempted to stab the needle into Jonathan's neck, but Jonathan managed to get a hand free to block the attack, stopping the needle point just centimeters away from his skin.

"Hello, yes police please, we have an armed burglar

in our house. Yes, he's still here. He's trying to kill my husband!" said a scared but controlled female voice.

"Police going to be here soon, Gazza, better finish the job," advised God.

Gary put all his weight on his needle arm, forcing the syringe to break the neck-skin of the man. One press of the plunger and the job would be done. But, before his brain could send the signal to his thumb, Gary felt a sharp pain in his head ripple through his body like a wave of blinding white light, knocking him off balance.

"Was it God?" Gary thought.

No, it was not God, it was Karen, hitting him in the skull with an unopened bottle of merlot.

Gary was off balance and stunned, giving Jonathan the space he needed to unpin himself from the wall and cabinet. He pushed Gary back, still blocking the vicar's syringe with his right hand. Then, Jonathan did something he had never done before. He head-butted the vicar, right in the eye.

"God give me strength," shouted Gary, gathering himself from the attack and trying again to force the syringe into the man's neck.

But now Jonathan had the leverage advantage and could defend himself. He parried Gary's syringe hand to the side and headbutted him again, this time in the mouth, busting up the holy-man's lip.

Gary staggered backwards from the blow. A searing

heat engulfed his face, his good eye filled with water and hot blood poured from his nose and mouth. He was losing the fight.

Another sharp pain to his head wracked his body. Karen had struck him with the merlot again. This time the bottle had shattered into shards of glass. Gary's arm went weak, and he dropped the syringe.

"I can't do this," said Gary.

"You must," insisted God.

"Give me strength."

"You already have it, my son."

Emboldened, Gary summoned his energy reserves. The situation was now desperate. Adrenaline pumped through his veins. He regained his balance, enough to swing a fist in the direction of the merlot. The punch clipped Karen in the face, sending her tumbling to the ground. Having bought himself some space, he scrambled to the floor in search of the syringe he had dropped, but before he could grab it, he felt himself being pulled out of the house by his dog collar.

He found himself outside, lying on his back. Some blurred faces stood over him. Gary tried to get to his feet, but as he did so he felt another blow to his head, sending him back to the floor. Stunned and concussed, he closed his eyes and went into a dreamland.

He awoke to see flashing lights and the barrel of a

taser pointed at his chest.

He closed his eyes again.

He was tired.

SOMEWHERE IN HEAVEN

Jesus's body lay in a burning heap.

The Demon retracted the fork and watched with curiosity as the fires on the holy robe burned out, leaving the material still intact.

Jesus groaned, then, with some struggle, got to his feet.

"Well, that hurt more than I expected. A lot more," he said as he felt the cauterised puncture wounds in his torso.

"What is your name, fallen Angel?"

The Demon looked at Jesus, more curious now the holy man had resurrected himself.

"Myy naaame isss Ssssmoke."

"Smoke? OK, well thank you Smoke. That went according to plan. I needed to witness the pain here and now I have. But tell me, what does your side get out of this?"

"Falssse hope. Makesss the sssuffering sssweeter."

"I see, well I'm glad I could help. I better be off now. Hopefully, we can do this again sometime?"

Smoke nodded and sculked away into the shadows of the tunnel.

Jesus waited until the Demon was out of sight, then opened a portal to Heaven and stepped through, arriving back in the thicket.

He took a big sniff of the fresh air and exhaled.

"That was intense," he said to himself.

His wounds still hurt. Creatures of Hell could wound and kill creatures of Heaven and vice versa. Jesus had the gift of resurrection but was not impervious to the pain Demon weapons inflicted, yet the experience in Hell had helped him temporarily purge some of his own troubled feelings, soothing the memories tormenting him from within.

He closed the portal behind him and went in search of a spring to bathe in.

Smoke watched from the shadows of Hell as Jesus closed the portal to Heaven. Just as the gateway shrank, he materialized from the darkness and lunged his fork into the portal, which was now only a few atoms thick, but still large enough to breach through to the other side. Smoke ripped open the gate with his Demon weapon and clambered through into Heaven.

He hid in the shadows of the thicket as the portal vanished behind him. His trick had worked; the portal had recognised the small chunks of holy flesh and blood, which had seared onto the flaming fork when he had impaled Jesus, fooling it into reopening and allowing him to breach through to the other side.

Smoke, a dark exile, a fallen Angel, had finally returned.

Smoke was home.

CHAPTER 7

Gary sat in his cold, dank cell.

His nose hurt. His lips were swollen. His back was stiff from the thin mattress.

He ran his fingers delicately over the back of his head, tenderly feeling the sharp bristle of the stitches that held together the sliced, lacerated wounds from the smashed wine bottle. Exploring further he discovered a small hard bump, he reasoned it must be a shard of glass that had burrowed into the skin.

His body ached. The assault had forced him to work unused muscles.

He was unfit.

Unbuilt for fighting.

At his core he was a man of peace, a pacifist. Yet he could no longer be those things. Not whilst under

God's instruction. Following the word of God, he was a man of violence, a man of death, a man of faith.

Staring vacantly at the wall opposite, grey and damp, he was reconnected to the world by a hammering on the cell door, followed by a curt female voice.

"Please stand up and prepare to exit the cell. Stand five feet away from the door."

He did what he was told.

The door thudded open and two officers entered the room.

"We're going to handcuff you, so, place your arms in front of you, with your hands together. Good."

The female officer handcuffed him. He found the brief touch of her hand against his wrist comforting as she locked the shackles.

"This way," she said as she led him out of the cell. A male officer followed in tow, ready to smash his head in with the extendable baton if he 'tried anything funny.' Disrespecting authority was not in his nature, but even if it was, his stitched-up cuts and swollen face dissuaded him from any inkling of disobedience.

He was led down the corridors of the police station to a small room.

"Please go in and sit down," she said gesturing to the armless chair in the back corner, facing the open door.

He went in and sat down.

"Wait here," she said, removing the cuffs and closing the door behind them, leaving him alone.

He was in an interview room, cold and small with neutral grey walls. A CCTV camera watched him from the corner of the ceiling. The table on his left had two tucked-in chairs and a large tape recorder.

There he waited. He stared at the closed door and disconnected from the outside world. His face sagged, mouth held slightly ajar, the tight swollen areas of his face relaxed.

An hour passed.

The door then opened with a shunt and two detectives walked in, snapping him back to reality.

They said nothing as they sat down in the chairs, positioning themselves between Gary and the door, cutting off the exit, a pressure tactic they used to unsettle suspects.

The man pressed the red button on the tape recorder. It made a screeching noise for 10 seconds then fell to a whisper of spinning wheels.

"Hello Mr Uxbridge," said the man, "I'm Detective Mackerel, and this is Detective Bracket. We're going to ask you a few questions today, OK?"

The detective paused, waiting for a response. Gary said nothing, but could feel them analyzing his body language, staring into his brain.

After a few moments, the detective continued; "For the record, Mr Uxbridge, this interview is being recorded for both audio and video. You do not have to say anything. But it may harm your defense if you do not mention when questioned something which you may later rely on in court. Anything you do say may be given in evidence.

"Do you know why you're being questioned today?"

Gary remained silent.

The detective exchanged a look with his colleague, then asked again.

"Mr Uxbridge, do you know why you're being questioned today?"

"No?" Gary mumbled, through a fat lip.

"How did you get those injuries?" Mackerel asked, observing the man's discomfort.

"I was assaulted," replied Gary, feebly, now gently touching his swollen eye.

"Who assaulted you, Gary?" asked Bracket, with a soft, sympathetic tone to her voice.

"A man… and a woman," Gary said slowly, moving his eyes to the right, giving the impression he was struggling to remember.

"Did you know these people?" Bracket followed up, her face expressing concern for his apparent injustice.

"No, I did not know them," Gary said pathetically.

"What did they do to you, Gary?" Mackerel asked gently, joining in with the fake concern for the vicar, allowing him to feel like the victim.

"Beat me, kicked me. Hit me with a bottle," Gary responded, feeling the bristles on his head with discomfort, turning his face to accentuate his wounds, bathing in the sympathy.

"Where did this happen?" Mackerel asked, hoping the suspect, now feeling a false sense of security, would declare themselves present at the crime scene.

"At their house," muttered Gary.

"Why were you at their house?" Mackerel continued.

"Sharing God's gift."

"Were you inside the house when this happened?" Bracket asked, still holding the soft, caring tone.

"Yes." Gary admitted.

"Why?" Mackerel asked, inquisitively.

"I was trying to save him," declared Gary, alluding to his innocence.

"Save him? Why were you trying to save him, Gary?" asked Bracket, still showing concern for Gary.

"God wants him in Heaven. To save him from this mortal realm. To save him from his disease."

"You mean, kill him?" Mackerel asked assertively, turning up the pressure.

"Save him. He had a disease of the soul, that he fought for so long, never surrendering to the urges to corrupt the innocent."

"What do you mean, Gary?" asked Bracket, now with a more serious note to her voice.

"The evil in his mind compelled him to lie with infants. But the light in his soul forbade him. He is tormented by conflict and yet never swayed to take the Devil's hand. The goodness in his heart remained unbroken. He resisted. Sacrificing his own needs so the innocent could be saved. It is time he is saved. That is what I was sent to do. End his mortal suffering so he can bathe for eternity in the light of the Holy Father. He was chosen by God to be saved, and I the savior."

"So, to be clear, you broke into his house to murder him because you thought he was a paedophile. But instead, he and his missus battered you to a pulp, put you flat on your arse, only to get arrested by us. Sound about right?" accused Mackerel, translating the vicar's words against him.

Gary didn't answer.

There was a knock on the interrogation room door.

"Excuse us for a few minutes," Mackerel stopped the tape and the detectives got up and left the room.

"What have we got?" Mackerel asked the evidence manager, Detective Dune.

"Toxicology report has come in about the lab found at the suspects residence."

"Great, what's he been cooking?"

"The active ingredients have similar chemical structures to 3-Methylfentanyl and Dimethyltryptamine," replied Dune as she read from the report.

Mackerel realised he may have overestimated his knowledge of narcotic chemical substances, which was limited to the odd line of MDMA he had sniffed as an undergraduate at student house parties.

"Meaning?"

"It is a blend of a lipophilic phenylpiperidine opioid agonist, and a serotonergic hallucinogen," answered Dune, still reading.

"English, please."

"It's a home brew cocktail of Fentanyl and DMT," Dune said, finally getting the hint, "Fentanyl is an ultra-potent opioid that gives users a powerful sense of euphoria. It's used as a pharmaceutical painkiller. It is highly addictive, and overdoses are common and often fatal when the drug is abused.

"DMT, on the other hand, is a high strength hallucinogenic that users experience as waking dreams. Tribal shamans are known to use it in rituals and claim it opens their minds to spirit dimensions and allows them to speak to aliens, higher powers and... deities."

"So basically, it's a homemade cocktail of heroin and

acid?" asked Mackerel, trying to relate the information to something tangible.

"Umm, not quite Macker," Bracket chipped in, "let's just say, if a 'heroin and acid concoction' was a Ferrari sports car, then this 'Fentanyl and DMT combo' is the fucking space shuttle!"

"OK, so its heavy. Dune, can we link it to the body?"

"Yes, lethal amounts of the cocktail were found in the blood of the deceased Julie McBride, and the pathologist confirms it is most certainly what caused her death, which was brain hypoxia by respiratory failure."

"That, my friend, is bloody great news! What about DNA matches, prints etc.?"

"Officers seized his clothes for forensics when he was in hospital, as you asked. So far, we can confirm the sole of his shoes match the footprints Fowley's team found on McBride's carpet, placing him at the scene. But we are still waiting on DNA comparisons."

"What about CCTV?"

"Detective Spark confirms her team have found footage showing Uxbridge's car leaving the vicinity at time of death."

"Excellent. How did Handy and Dubois get on with interviewing the husband?"

"Husband has an alibi and no motive, he's clean, and let's just say Dubois was his usual charming self."

"Great, we can eliminate him as a suspect. June, thank you. Brackett let's get a coffee, go through the notes, review our interview strategy and have Uxbridge stew a bit longer."

"Oh, Stephen, one more thing. When Uxbridge was unconscious in hospital, the Doctors examined him and found track marks between his toes. They took a blood sample and found small traces of 'the cocktail' in his system."

Bracket and Mackerel looked at each other.

"He's been using!" they said in unison.

SOMEWHERE
IN HEAVEN

Julie McBride sat on a beach with white sand and a shimmering white sea.

She was happy.

She wiggled her toes, burrowing them into the soft white diamond grains and marveled at the pleasure as they caressed her skin like liquid silk.

The white sun warmed her face with a pleasing glow as she watched waves that made no sound. Just silence, tranquility, bliss.

Minutes or hours passed until her peace was upended and replaced by a new one.

A figure had emerged, some distance away from her on the beach. Another soul, here to enjoy the isolation.

The figure grew larger as it moved towards her until it was close enough for Julie to make out its details.

It was a woman that looked to be in their early twenties. The figure was fit and lean with athletic beauty. She was carrying a spear and wore an animalistic snarl contorted across her face.

Julie could sense the impending confrontation. This awareness was rewarded with the typical feelings of heavenly bliss and joyful excitement.

Julie rose to her feet and at that instant the spear wielding athlete charged at her, its vocal cords sounded a long, crackling shriek of a war-cry, that Julie heard as a divinely soothing serenade.

As the warrior woman drove the spear at her torso, Julie had a perplexing thought: she knew that if the spear pierced her body, she would experience the implicit pain as divine pleasure, true euphoric bliss. On the other hand, if she chose to defend herself, turn the spear onto the assailant, thus interrupting this other soul's expression of holy freedom, Julie would still feel the same sensation of bliss that she would have had she succumb to the attack, as would the warrior woman.

Whatever the outcome, good or bad, she was now programmed to not only accept it, but enjoy it and be blissfully rewarded by it. They all were. All souls in Heaven.

She recognised that this was how all these identities, with all their distinct hopes and dreams, feelings and desires, shared the same existence harmoniously.

Acceptance.

No experience of pain or suffering could ever be felt. Only pleasure.

And with this realisation, the perplexing thought took root and became a splinter in her mind.

What if Julie wanted to feel disdain and anger?

What if she wanted to feel pain, just to know that she could?

What if she didn't want to share Heaven with other souls, so she could sit on this beach undisturbed and alone.

It was the fact that she was not bothered about being bothered, that bothered her. A contradiction of freewill, that she had somehow kept and lost simultaneously.

She grabbed the spear thrusted by the shrieking woman, just before the metal tip had reached her exposed belly, and, with inhuman strength, ripped it from the warrior's grasp, span it around and with an upwards thrust, stabbed the spear through the woman's soft under skin of her chin and out the back of her head. She then dug the hilt of the spear into the sand so that the warrior woman dangled a foot from the ground, impaled like a trophy wrack.

As expected from the result of this action, a liquid pleasure, forever novel coursed through her veins like a drug.

She sat back down and looked over the sea, back to tranquility. Yet the splinter in her mind remained, forming small cracks around it.

As she chewed over this complication, she watched the twinkling silhouette of a flock of Angels pass in front of the white sun on the horizon.

It was as if all the souls and her were the guest residents at a luxury resort, and the Angels, staff that had always been there.

Was this why the Human souls never bothered to attack the Angels like they did each other? Out of respect for authority and hierarchy. Did the Angels have a unique experience of Heaven, did they feel something higher?

As her mind wandered, the cracks grew. And in those cracks, dark possibilities and questions formed.

Could she catch an Angel?

Could she kill one?

Could she become one?

CHAPTER 8

Mackerel clicked record on the tape recorder, took a sip of coffee from his paper cup and smiled politely while the speakers wailed a high pitch squeal for about 10 seconds.

Once the recorder had silenced to a mechanical hum, Mackerel stated the time, date, and names of parties in the room.

He took another sip of coffee and placed it back on the table. Bracket and he were armed with new evidence and a revised strategy.

He would turn up the heat with the accusations, Bracket would continue to observe the body language, measure speech patterns, and cross-reference responses with their new evidence.

They had him for Jonathan, now they needed a confession for the murder of Julie McBride.

"Did you kill Julie McBride?"

"Yes."

"Fuck me, that was easy!" Mackerel thought to himself. He resisted looking at Bracket to his left, not wanting to give away his surprise.

"Why did you kill Julie McBride?"

"To save her."

"Save her from what?"

"A mortal life. She's in Heaven now."

"Boom, three questions in and I got the confession. That must be a record," thought Mackerel.

"OK thank you, Gary."

"I want to ask about the drug you used to kill Mrs McBride. How did you get it?"

"I made it."

"How? Is that what the chemistry set is for, the one we found at your flat?"

Gary paused then answered, "Yes."

"Our scientists tell me it's quite a complicated job making what you made. I have read your background and don't see any history of chemistry in your academic profile, no traces of research on your computer. How did you know what to do, did someone help you?"

"Yes."

"Can you tell me their name?"

"God."

"Fucking 'God shit' again," Mackerel thought to himself, "how does God help you?" he asked, hiding his frustration.

"He told me how to do it."

"How, through a beam of light, an Angel?"

"No, he told me directly, I heard his voice, felt his divine presence."

Mackerel thought for a moment. Uxbridge most certainly had traces of DMT in his system, so could quite plausibly have hallucinated this God character. But, on the other hand, maybe Gary had a handler that referred to themselves God. It would fit the religious extremist/ cultist pattern; shadowy character brainwashes susceptible individual into performing an atrocity, gets them hooked on mind-altering drugs to believe the handler's lies.

He continued with his line of inquiry, whatever the angle, Uxbridge was incriminating himself on record.

"So, what, God talked you through it?"

"Yes."

"Where did you get the ingredients and apparatus?"

"I made them."

"You made the glass tubes? So, you're an engineer now? Let me guess, God gave you the instructions?

"He did."

"And the ingredients? Those are illegal base chemicals you used, did God teach you how to pull them out your arse?"

Mackerel could not help feeling like the vicar was lying, protecting someone. He decided to change tack, he wanted to get Gary on motive and ability to commit the crime, which would add credibility to the confession.

"Why did you clean the scene, Gary?"

"God told me too."

"Why? So you wouldn't be caught? So you could kill again?"

"You would interfere with God's plan. He wants to save people, send them to Heaven. You would stop that and keep them trapped in mortality, keep them enslaved. Your attempt to stop me is an attempt to stop God. You cannot stop God, for He is everything, He is power."

"Well, a lady with a wine bottle stopped you mate. I thought you were God's boy. He doesn't seem to have your back now, does he?"

"God does have my back. He's with me right now."

"Oh yeah, is that right?"

"Yes, and he knows all about you Detective Steven Mackerel."

Mackerel decided to bite.

"What does he know?"

Gary's facial expression changed. His eyes partially rolled upwards, his muscles relaxed letting his busted jaw go limp and ajar, like he was in the first half of a yawn.

"Your name is Stephen James Mackerel. You were born 10th June 1987. You joined the police in your late 20's via the controversial Detective Fast Track Program available only to university graduates, thus enabling you to skip years of police graft to acquire your current position. You have completed your PIP level 3 exams and are awaiting the official promotion to the rank of Detective Chief Inspector, even though you are currently working in that capacity on this case. This has led to feelings of resentment from your peers, who express their disdain towards you passive-aggressively on a daily basis. You earn £54,000 a year. You live alone. You are alo-"

"OK, very good, Gary. So, God *really is* whispering in your ear then," Mackerel interrupted, with a dose of sarcasm."

"Only one problem. I was born 10th of June 1985, not 1987. So, it seems like your God made a mistake, doesn't it?"

Gary snapped out his trance and stared at the detective in disbelief, trying to calculate what the detective was up to. Was the detective telling the truth, had God fed him misinformation, was he indeed mad after all?

Mackerel was bluffing about the incorrect birth year

to unsettle Gary. The vicar had stated the facts correctly, amazingly. Though Mackerel suspected Uxbridge had gotten access to his police personal file, somehow.

Bracket scribbled away in her pad. Noting the strange event down.

Mackerel changed the subject whilst he had the vicar on the back foot.

"How do you know Julie McBride?"

"She was a member of my church."

Bracket pulled out a note from the first interview and showed it to Mackerel, he acknowledged and followed up.

"Why did you target her? Was it like with your second victim, Jonathan, does it have something to do with hurting kids?

"It's true, Julie had the desire to kill her infant. She was tired and alone, but she chose God's selfless love, she allowed her child to live. God sees the good in her, he chose her to be saved."

Bracket wrote it down and pulled out a photo from the crime scene and placed it on the table for Gary to see.

"You see this picture of Julie; she has a cut on her forehead. How did she get that, Gary?" asked Bracket.

"She resisted."

"You mean she resisted being murdered, so, you hit her and tied her to the chair?" Mackerel retorted.

"Yes, she was rejecting God's gift."

"Is that what you call the drugs you made, 'God's Gift?'"

Gary didn't answer.

"What if she didn't want this 'gift', Gary. Surely it's her choice to accept it or not?"

"She didn't have a choice. She was going to die eventually either by accident or disease, or time. I was saving her from that terrible fate by giving her a humane passage."

"And Jonathan, the man you attacked last night, was his death inevitable too?"

"All death is inevitable."

"Why not just let them die then?"

"God has devised a better way, a blissful shortcut for the souls destined for Heaven, bypassing the natural torment of mortal life and death. That is God's gift."

"So, what, he sends you to inject them with a syringe full of hallucinogenic super smack? I mean, I get that you use the Fentanyl to incapacitate the victims and give them sense of euphoria as they overdose, but why the hallucinogen, why the DMT?"

Gary paused, then answered, "because it opens their minds to God. They see the Heaven that awaits them, and they pass fearlessly from mortality."

"Is this how you opened your mind to God, by using the drugs yourself?"

"I'm a vicar, detective. My mind was always open to God."

"Why are you confessing today?"

"To dismiss the will of God would be a sin. God protects me. The law will recognise I do God's work."

"Poor guy, he'd been sold some shit alright," Mackerel thought, yet the detective was very aware that the vicar might be playing for insanity or covering for a handler.

"Do we have enough?" Mackerel asked Bracket.

"Yes," Bracket nodded.

"OK, Mr Uxbridge, I am formally charging you with the premeditated murder of Mrs Julie McBride as well as the attempted murder of Mr Jonathan Foot."

SOMEWHERE IN HEAVEN

Julie McBride raced through the woods. Mud and twigs kicked up from the studded rear tire as the motor of the scrambler bike barked and snarled with fuel injected ferocity.

She was chasing a flock of Angels headed east at pace. She assumed they were off for another ceremony of brutality.

On her person she carried the spear she had claimed as trophy from the shrieking warrior woman, a rope net, and an Uzi 9mm sub machine gun.

She was determined to kill an Angel, just to see if she could. And, maybe with that act, she could ascend.

She carved through the trail, keeping an eye on the sky, keeping the Angel silhouettes in sight.

She enjoyed riding the bike. She had always wanted to ride when she was a mortal on earth before she died, but she never got around to it. Single parent life did not afford her the time, money, nor energy. Now she was thankful for the opportunity.

She zoomed past trees, mud, and thickets.

She rode past mutilated bodies, impaled on tree branches, rotting and decomposing, ready to rematerialize wherever the soul's subconsciousness saw fit, as her soul had, many times over.

She rode past wild animals, bizarre versions of their earthly selves, shifting forms continuously in undecided states of evolution, only to be scared away by the growl of the bike engine, leaving shaking flora as the only evidence of their presence.

She shot out of the woods and into a majestic clearing as she gained on the flock, which now hovered in place above the tree line some distance away.

They appeared to have spotted something on the ground.

Then an Angel from the flock fell from the sky.

CHAPTER 9

"Well, that was fucking mental. Do you think he's actually 'proper crazy?'" Mackerel asked Bracket.

"Not sure, do you think he had help?" she replied, scooping up some rice and sauce.

"Yes..." Mackerel said as he glugged some beer.

"So, you think he's playing us?" Bracket sipped her beer.

"Possibly. He either believes actual 'God' is helping him, or he wants us to *think* he believes 'God' is helping him, so we think he's crazy... or, he has a handler who uses the codename 'God', the latter meaning we'd need to track down this handler and quickly."

"Pretty amazing how he knew that stuff about you?"

"Yeah, he must have hacked my file somehow."

"Have you ever considered that God does exist?"

"You're not telling me you believe him, that God, as in the 'Great Almighty', is actually helping this lunatic?"

"Of course not, but it's interesting to speculate isn't it. For instance, what if God does exist and Uxbridge is doing God's work? Would that mean we are actively working against the will of God by stopping Uxbridge?" Bracket mused swigging more beer and staring philosophically at the ceiling.

"If that was true, then firstly, God is an arsehole who has condoned the terrorizing of innocent people while simultaneously condemning Uxbridge to an inevitably horrible life in prison. Secondly, this is England, a democratic secular society. The church and thus God has no jurisdiction in our legal system, and, if God doesn't like that, if God wants to roll back the enlightenment period, then God needs to contact his local motherfuckin' MP!" Mackerel scooped a forkful of Jalfrezi into his mouth and gulped another swig of Tiger beer.

Bracket dunked a shard of poppadum into the various chutneys, adding to the cross contamination of flavors.

She watched as Mackerel shoveled more curry into his gob.

"You're not scared then?" she quizzed.

"Scared of what?"

"Uh, eternal damnation?"

"I'm an atheist, I don't believe in that shit. But if I were to be judged...then I hope I would be judged on the choices I made in the circumstances I made them. My task is simple; catch the people who hurt others and gather the evidence needed to stand up in court and put them away. If God wants to punish me for catching a murderer, then so be it, at least I've done my job." Mackerel mopped his plate with half an onion bhaji.

"Do you think the judge will put him in the 'Crazy Can?'"

"Not sure. He has confessed, shown no remorse and seems fully paid up to the religious assassination idea. But he prepared a deadly drug, committed the murder then wiped the scene clean so he could attack a second victim. That shows a sound enough mind to know to avoid getting caught. This guy was going to do it again and again... we just stopped a serial killer..."

"Are stopping. He ain't locked up yet. We need to make sure he doesn't walk," Bracket pointed out.

"Ava will make sure he doesn't." assured Mackerel.

"Too right, is she coming down or what? We'll be finished if she doesn't get a groove on," Bracket noted, observing their half-eaten curries.

A few minutes later, Ava Étranger walked into the curry house and scanned the room.

Bracket gave her a smile and a wave, getting her

attention.

"Hi guys, sorry I took so long."

"No worries, sorry we started without you."

"Ah that's fine. I ate on the journey"

"Well, great to see you," said Bracket.

"So... who's the judge?" Mackerel asked, cutting to the chase.

"Judge Thomas."

"Is that good for us?"

"Uncertain. He's one of those 'modern progressive' types. 'New school.'"

"Meaning?"

"Meaning, Thomas advocates criminal rehabilitation. He's been known to give lenient sentences based on cooperation and remorse. He can see the potential in a defendant, that they can be reintegrated back into society. He also believes in mental illness and that sometimes prison isn't the best place for their rehabilitation. He can be seen as soft, by some. But he's smart and fair."

"So, what about our case?" asked Bracket, raising her hand to get the waiters attention, "three Tigers, please," she asked the waiter.

"Oh, not for me I'm driving," Étranger said, waving her hand.

"Well, about your case, if the evidence is as good as

you say it is, no problem...we just need to build the story, and not give Thomas and the jury *any* reason to think that Gary was delusional to the point he didn't know wrong from right, at the time of the crimes."

"What about the religious extremism, terrorism angle, shall we go with that?"

"I'd say, no. Your evidence for that is speculative at best. Saying the Church of England is an ideology used by terrorists is not going to sit well without absolute proof. There would be public outrage at the accusation, and, you would be slinging shit at immensely powerful people, The Queen for instance."

"What if we get the proof?"

"If you get the proof, then give me a call...but right now, we don't want the Crown Court, the press and the public distracted from the evidence we do have, which is currently an open and shut case. We are stronger if the story says that he was working alone, that he is a cold-blooded killer who uses religion simply as a tool to get close to his victims. You have the evidence for that, and the motive."

"OK, what about the fact he's sticking with the 'God told me to do it' story. That's a ticket to the 'Crazy Can,' right? He could be out in a few years by simply playing the 'I'm sane now' card?" asked Mackerel.

"Don't worry, I know a highly respected Forensic Psychologist, who has given me a written evaluation on Gary's mental health. We can use it in court as a 'Subject Matter Expert' statement, which we can weave into our narrative. We also have Gary's blood sample statement proving he used hallucinogens. But as it doesn't reveal the *exact* time he used; we couldn't say for a fact that he was on drugs at the time he committed the crime, only that he used sometime within the 72 hours prior. But as hallucinogen's are known to trigger psychotic episodes in certain types of people, and as 'drugs made me crazy' is not a favourable legal defense, we can keep it in our back pocket in case we need it."

"OK, so it's agreed then. We'll drop the 'terrorist cell/ handler' angle, for now, and run with the 'cold-blooded serial killer' narrative. We're trusting you on this Ava. Do not let him walk."

"Don't worry, your team has done a bloody decent job, now let me do mine," she smiled, "this is what I do."

SOMEWHERE
IN HEAVEN

Smoke flew fast and close to the ground, batting his wings with powerful strokes between glides, aiming for the tree line.

He checked over his shoulder, had he lost them?

No.

The posse of Angels was still on his tail, glowing gold with righteous indignation.

He made it to the woods and weaved with slalom speed through the tree trunks.

Two members of the group chased after him as the others flew above the treetops, scouting for exit points.

He saw shade ahead, shadows large enough to hide

in, but he needed to conceal his planned destination to his pursuers.

Smoke shot passed the shadows and then doubled back, flying in a figure of eight through the trees.

Arriving with a few seconds to spare, the Demon Angel merged with the shadow at its darkest point, which was in a knot of giant tree roots, sheltered by a thick canopy overhead.

Moments later one Angel flew by the hiding place and disappeared into the thick of the woods. The other, shrewder Angel tracked the figure of eight a second time before landing at the edge of the shadow, its glow illuminating the darkness around it.

It scanned the area suspiciously and stepped closer towards the root. The shadows moved and shrunk against the Angel's luminescence, but Smoke, a skilled shade shifter, was able to warp, curve and bend with the transient dark.

Staring at the shroud, directly where Smoke was hidden, the Angel, sensing evil, began to draw its sword. Suddenly a sound far in the distance caught its attention. It hesitated for a second, then in a flash of speed it sheathed its weapon and shot off in pursuit, returning the area to shade.

After some time, Smoke emerged from the shadows.

Had he lost them?

Yes, for now.

He stalked cautiously through the wood, looking for any Angels waiting in ambush, when a gold glow stealing out from some bushes caught his eye.

Readying his hell-fork for combat, he slowly approached the flora.

There was no reaction to his approach, no movement, yet the gold light still shone.

Coiled like a viper, he lunged his hell-fork violently into the bush, hitting what felt like solid metal. Curious he ripped away the leaves and found a motorbike resting on its side, an amber glow projecting from its single headlight. At that moment, a net dropped from the treetops above and entangled him.

Trapped and surprised, he turned in the direction of the footsteps fast approaching and saw a human soul charging towards him.

He tried to tear and cut his way free from the net, but his body shook uncontrollably with the shocks of impact. Julie was emptying a full clip of fully automatic holy bullets into him from the Uzi 9mm.

Finally breaking through the net, wounded and with shredded wings, Smoke attempted to take off and escape the devastating sneak attack.

Julie, anticipating the 'Angel's' attempt to flee, leapt head-height into the air and launched the spear down, impaling Smoke to the ground.

She stood over the deformed, ashen Angel, writhing in pain.

She had never seen one like this before. It did not glow with a golden radiance like the others.

But there must be a light somewhere inside of it, a light she could consume.

How else was she to ascend?

She ripped open its chest and shadow erupted from the cavity.

Darkness engulfed her.

And she began to eat.

CHAPTER 10

Wearing his black gown, His Honor Judge Thomas lifted his eyes from the case documents he was reviewing and observed the room.

"Please stand."

The room stood.

"The defendant, Mr Uxbridge has chosen to plead 'not guilty'. Now that the jury has been sworn in, it is time for the prosecution to present their case against Mr Uxbridge. Once that is complete, the defense will have the opportunity to refute any claims made against them."

He looked at Ava Étranger.

"Are you ready to proceed?"

"Yes, Your Honor."

Ava turned to the jury.

"We are here today to prosecute Gary Uxbridge for the cold-blooded murder of a Mrs Julie McBride, and the attempted murder of a Mr Jonathan Foot. Mr Uxbridge is a malicious killer who uses religion not only to condone and shield himself from the responsibility of his terrible actions, but also to gain the trust of his victims. Blinding them to the danger they faced.

"He is a ruthless and calculating killer who has gone to great lengths in planning and covering up his crimes. He would most likely kill again if we had not caught him. The defense will try and persuade you of the defendant's good character, lack of previous offences and mental health condition. This will be to win him a reduced sentence or relocation from prison to a secure hospital, where his conditions may be more favorable.

"Today we will be presenting evidence that will confirm without question the defendant's guilt of the crimes committed and his cerebral clarity to carry out those crimes. The evidence presented will be in the form of forensic images and reports, CCTV imagery, signed witness statements, and subject matter expert statements. You will each receive a pack containing the evidence presented here today." Ava studied the reactions of the jury, gauging the impact of her opening statement.

She turned to Judge Thomas.

"Your Honor, I request permission to present the

prosecution's evidence."

"You may proceed."

"Thank you, Your Honor. First, I would like to present to the jury some forensic images of the murder scene."

She nodded to the court administrator who fired up the projector, which blared an image onto the pull-down whiteboard.

"Here is Julie McBride, deceased, as she was found," Ava informed the jury.

She gestured to the image.

"Notice her position. She is sitting in her chair by the window, hands on each arm rest. Notice she seems peaceful and relaxed, as if she has died in her sleep, on her favorite chair."

She pulled up another slide.

"These are photos of the interior of the house, the sitting room, kitchen, and hallways. Notice the cleanliness, nothing on the sides, and the floor has been wiped clean. This could be considered normal for a middle-aged woman living by herself."

She clicked to the next slide, back to Julie McBride.

"Remember, this is a murder scene. There is no sign of forced entry, no sign of a struggle, no sign of resistance. This was by way of design by the killer, whose intention was to make the murder appear like a natural death to whoever found the victim.

"More so, the room was wiped clean by the killer, an attempt to dispose of incriminating evidence, so to slow down and misdirect the police and to enable the killer to escape justice and target further victims. But despite their best efforts, the killer could not mask their crime."

She clicked to the next slide, composed of two forensic images.

"Here you can see a small abrasion on the brow of the victim. On the second image, a small red scratch on the wrist."

She held up a document.

"This is what the forensic pathologist report states about these wounds:

Regarding the wound on the brow, this type of injury is caused by blunt force trauma, possibly by a punch. The wound on the wrist is an intravenous wound consistent with the damage to skin caused by a needle injection. These wounds likely happened at the same time of each other, within one hour.

"The victim was punched in the face and injected in the wrist with a needle."

Ava clicked to the next slide, showing an image of the back of the chair where the victim sat, an image showing a close-up of the deceased's upper torso, the victim's fingernails and a sock.

"Here you will notice the back of the chair, notice the pale stripes across the upper middle area. As per section 2 of your document, forensic evidence states these stripes are caused by the removal of adhesive tape from the fabric, removing dust and a layer of the material. Note the use of the word 'tape.'

"The pathologist states that during the autopsy:

The victim had vibices in the form of pale stripes on the upper torso and arms, caused by abnormal external pressure, creating a lack of blood flow in those parts of the body at time of death.

"The vibices on the body are the same size as the tape marks found on the chair. This evidence proves the victim was restrained.

"Notice image 7. The bundle of socks; they were found in the victim's kitchen bin. The victim's saliva was found on these socks. In addition, small particles of the same sock fabric were found at the opening of the victim's mouth, the back of the mouth and in the throat. The socks were, within an hour to time of death, in the victim's mouth and throat area.

"Finally, the forensic pathologist states that the cause of death was by 'brain hypoxia', caused by a 'chemical agent injected into the victim's blood stream, which induced respiratory failure'.

"The evidence concludes the victim was beaten, gagged, tied to a chair, then injected with a deadly substance that suffocated her, ending her life. The scene was then cleaned to dispose of any incriminating evidence."

Ava clicked back to the original image of Julie, as she was found, peacefully deceased on her front room chair.

"What this shows, is a careful and intentional attempt by the culprit to commit murder and then conceal the act. Such activities carried out are not that of one experiencing the frenzy of a psychotic episode, but that of a cold and calculated killer.

"So, what does this have to do with our defendant, what evidence if any, puts them at the scene of the crime? For that I can say, on the surface there is little, as one would be expecting from a scene wiped of evidence. However, our forensic team is thorough, and all criminals make mistakes.

"Next slide, please."

The image of Julie McBride's hands appeared on the screen.

"The victim was found to have small amounts of foreign skin particles and blood under the fingernails of her right hand. We believe the victim had scratched her attacker on the wrist during the assault, leaving traces of the attacker's DNA under her fingernails.

"We analysed the blood and tissue samples found under the victim's nails and found that the DNA is a direct match to that of the defendant, Mr Uxbridge.

"If that wasn't evidence enough, Julie's DNA was found on a pair of leather gloves that were in the possession of the defendant."

Ava pulled up a new slide, this time displaying a table of evidence.

"Here is a collection of evidence found on the person of the defendant and seized from the defendants place of residence. We have the murder weapon: a hypodermic needle and syringe, containing traces of the victim's DNA and the same toxic agent responsible for Julie's death. We have a chemistry lab, found at the defendant's place of residence, which was used to manufacture the agent that killed Julie McBride.

"The documents handed to you contain the exhaustive list of evidence that proves the defendant's guilt, which includes shoe impressions, CCTV surveillance, tire prints and witness accounts...

"So, what about motive? Why did the defendant murder Julie McBride?

"In one of many police interviews with the suspect, Gary stated he was 'sending Julie to Heaven' because 'she wanted to kill her baby'.

"He murdered Julie because he believed she wanted to commit infanticide. Which is, in religious terms, regarded as a great sin. The defendant, a vicar for the Church of England carried out this attack as retribution for this "sin" by murdering her.

"This sentiment is repeated in the attempted murder of Jonathan Foot. After murdering Julie McBride, the defendant wasted no time tracking down his next victim. This time crossing county lines, in an attempt to throw detectives off the scent.

"Once again, he used his religious status as tool to get access to the victim, Mr Foot. But this time he was unable to dupe Mr Foot into inviting him into their place of residence. Failing to earn the victim's trust, the defendant revealed his true intentions, breaking into the property and assaulting Mr Foot, then attempting to inject the Mr Foot with the same deadly agent that killed his previous victim, the aforementioned Julie McBride.

"Thankfully, the victim and his spouse were able to fight off the defendant and with help from concerned neighbours, were able to restrain the suspect until the police arrived.

"In a witness testimony, Mr Foot stated Gary had accused him of being a paedophile and that he was doing God's work by ending the victim's life. This was repeated by the defendant during one of many interrogations with detectives.

"Note that once again, the suspect used religion as a cloak to earn a victims trust, and once again was targeting victims on his belief that they were wishing to harm children.

"The suspect, the pattern of their crimes and their motives have been analysed by a Forensic Phycologist, who holds the role of Subject Matter Expert for the prosecution. Here is an excerpt from their statement:

The suspects multiple cases of using unfounded accusations of infanticide against their victims is a clear example of the suspect intentionally projecting their own inner desires and fantasies of harming minors onto the victim.

Because the suspect's fantasies are in direct conflict with the religious belief system that the suspect subscribes to, they wish to punish themselves for those fantasies.

But, for the suspect, these desires they wish to purge exist in an abstract and intangible form, so they project these 'sins' onto the 'other,' thus externalizing the thoughts and giving them a tangible object to punish.

They believe that by attributing their victim with these properties and killing them, they are thus killing that part of themselves that have the fantasies, relieving the suspect of their sense of sin.

"He then states:

This phenomenon should not be considered a delusion or an act of insanity - described as a defendant not in control of their actions due to the onset of psychosis - as the person acting out this process understands the underlying reasons for doing so.

Therefore, they go to such lengths to plan and conceal their crimes, and use positions of power to attract vulnerable victims, who put up little resistance until it's too late, because they, the suspect, ultimately know that what they are doing is wrong."

Ava observed the jury as the information settled in.

"To conclude, we have presented here today evidence and motive that the defendant is responsible for the murder of Julie McBride.

"We have provided evidence and witness testimonials to the attempted murder of Mr Foot.

"We have shown that the cases are linked and have provided reason and evidence that the defendant was sane during the events and that they exploited religion as a weapon to commit these acts.

"As such, all evidence, witness accounts and transcripts used today are available in the packs you have been given."

Ava looked at the jury and studied their reactions, then at the Judge.

"Does the prosecution wish to present any further evidence," said His Honor Thomas.

"No, Your Honor, the prosecution rests."

"Thank you, Mrs Étranger. We will take a twenty-minute break, then proceed with the defense hearing. Court adjourned."

SOMEWHERE
IN HEAVEN

The four hunter Angels lay in the dirt, stiff and dull, wearing agonised expressions, arranged head to toe in a perfect square. Each eviscerated.

At the center of the geometry stood the new Angel-Demon. Part Heavenly soul, part Fallen Angel of Hell.

Julie inhaled the experience. The metamorphosis. She could feel everything now; pleasure, pain, love, hate. Power.

She didn't glow with golden radiance like the Angels, nor was she burned ash white and heavily scarred like the Demon, she was just... normal, as she was before. Her new wings feathered crow black.

She took off into the sky, above the tree line, then

further up into the clouds, soaring majestically. She glided, barrel rolled and dived, she hovered and back flipped, learning her new wings, feeling the exhilaration of flight.

She had ascended. Balanced. Human amplified.

The splinter in her mind festered now.

She had killed and consumed Angels of Heaven and Hell. She had transformed. Could she transform further? What were the limits? What was in the realm of possibility, here, now?

Her imagination stretched.

Could she kill God?

Could she consume it?

Could she become it?

And with that thought she merged with darkness.

CHAPTER 11

Mr Uxbridge, we understand you have now chosen to represent yourself. Do you have anything to say in your defense?

"I do not represent myself I represent God. I did what I did under God's guidance. Mrs McBride is in Heaven now. She is saved. We saved her from this mortal life. Why don't you understand this? Why don't you understand that what I did for her, what I tried to do for Jonathan…it was holy, it was pure. It was God's will to have them go home."

Judge Thomas sighed and gestured to Ava.

"Would you like to cross examine the witness."

"No, Your Honor," Ava declined, knowing she had won.

"The jury will now leave to consider the verdict," instructed Judge Thomas, looking back at his notes, as the jury stood up and left the courtroom.

30 minutes later the jury returned to their seats, only the lead juror stood. The courtroom fell silent.

"Have you come to a unanimous verdict, or does the jury require more time?"

"We have come to a unanimous verdict, Your Honor."

"And what is that verdict."

"We find the defendant, Mr Gary Uxbridge, guilty of all charges."

"Mr Uxbridge, having been convicted, it is now time to pass sentence. I have reviewed your case and taken into consideration the aggravating and mitigating factors presented to me throughout. This includes your lack of criminal record and a review of your mental health, as well as the nature of the crimes and the method in which those crimes were committed. As such, the following sentences I believe are fair to the proportion and severity of the crimes, as of British law.

"Mr Gary Uxbridge, you are sentenced to a whole life term in prison without parole for the premeditated murder of Mrs Julie McBride.

"You are sentenced to thirty years in prison for the attempted murder of Mr Jonathan Foot.

"You are sentenced to two years in prison for the aggravated assault of Mrs Karen Foot.

"You are sentenced to ten years in prison for the illegal manufacture of a deadly narcotic.

"These sentences will run consecutively.

"It is without a doubt, Gary Uxbridge, that you are a devious and dangerous individual who has planned and executed these terrible crimes without remorse for the victims or their families. It is clear, that without intervention, you would have gone on to kill again and again.

"Even though you have admitted to your crimes during police interviews, you still attribute responsibility to God rather than to yourself. You have defecated on the good name of the Church; its values and the important work the institution does in the name of kindness and peace. You have bastardised the message of God that you claim to serve, but most importantly you have betrayed the lives of the very people who look to you for guidance. You have no place in society and will spend the rest of your days behind bars."

Gary stared at the Judge. Tears ran down his face and he wept.

"I tried My Lord. What do we do now?" he asked God.

"Uh, well, about that. You didn't complete your mission, and now it looks like you never will. You can't really help me anymore."

"Please, God, please, I did what you asked."

"Look Gary, I just can't use you mate. I thought I could, I thought you were made of the right stuff, but, well…."

"I tried, please, just give me another chance, I beg of you."

"Mate, the best I can do is have a word with the other side and make sure you don't go to Hell for the murder. Julie did come back to Heaven after all. But, quid pro quo, rules being rules, if you're not going Hell, you won't be coming to Heaven either. If Lucifer can't have you, then neither can I."

"Wait…what! I'm not allowed into Heaven?"

"Afraid not mate, sorry…but you're not going to Hell either, so that's a plus. Think of it like spiritual diplomatic immunity, my gift to you. You're a free man, so to speak."

"So, where do I go when I die?"

"Nowhere. You just die. Anyway, I hope you understand, I can't be seen to have anything to do with you anymore. No hard feelings, yeah?"

"Please God, please don't leave me, not after everything we've been through."

"Sorry bro, it's done. Have a good one, yeah? Enjoy your new freedom. Peace-out!"

And like that God was gone.

Gary was left with just the static of his own mind.

He awoke from his trance and was in the courtroom, the Judge still talking.

"No! I'm sorry! It was me, all me, it wasn't God. I'm so sorry for the things I've done in God's name. It was wrong. Please reconsider Your Honor," Gary pleaded, suddenly feeling very alone.

Judge Thomas looked at him with a frown.

"You've had plenty of opportunities for remorse Mr Uxbridge. You are not the first person to experience regret once judgement has been passed.

"Take him away."

Ava watched as Gary was led away in cuffs, sobbing pathetically. She exited the courtroom and pulled out her phone.

"Yep, yep, great news Ava! You're a legend!" Mackerel put away his mobile, "guys, the calls just come in, Thomas gave him life without parole, Étranger did it!"

"Congratulations Mackerel! You got the bastard!"

Mackerel and Bracket were greeted with the applause of a cheering standing ovation.

"I'm not a hero. Just a regular guy doing my job." Mackerel thanked in a pho-gruff mock American accent, "besides, I couldn't have done it without you guys and Birmingham here," he said patting Bracket on the back.

"You've done very well, both of you. Uxbridge is a real nasty piece of work, and he may well have slipped under the radar if it wasn't for your professionalism, quick thinking and damn fine police work," said Chief Superintendent Hari Spencer, giving Mackerel and Bracket a sincere smile.

The hero detectives said their Thank-Yous then Mackerel took the opportunity to catch up with Spencer.

"Chief, have you got a few secs?" Mackerel asked discreetly.

"Sure, what is it, Stephen?"

"I was wondering, as I've passed my exams, and just bagged a potential serial killer, perhaps I could get that promotion to DCI?"

"Well, Stephen, there would be a lot of competition for that position if it were available. However, your performance has been noted."

"OK, thank you, Chief," Mackerel said, hiding his disappointment.

"Let's see how you get on running the G.H.U task-force for now, deputy," Spencer said, winking with a smile before walking off.

"What did she say?" whispered Bracket.

"I think I've just been made deputy SIO," Mackerel whispered back, grinning.

A brief time later, Mackerel gathered with the other detectives, holding drinks in plastic cups, cigarette smoke blowing out an open window.

"We got our man. That's a win. Another scumbag off the streets, right? Now, we could put it to bed and move on. We could. We charged Uxbridge as a lone wolf, an anomaly, a random psycho killer. Why? Because that's the only hard evidence we had to get the sentence we did. But we know Gary Uxbridge and I am convinced that there is no way he was working alone.

"How do I know this, what examples am I talking about? How about the complex homemade drugs lab in his living room, or his seemingly intimate knowledge of his victims, especially Jonathan, whom he'd never met. Remember Gary accused Jonathan of being a 'paedo,' well I did some digging in my spare time and guess what popped up, Jonathan's Foot's medical records show he had indeed sought medical help for his sexual desires towards minors, just like Uxbridge had claimed.

"So how the fuck did Uxbridge get hold of the victim's confidential medical records? We know Gary isn't that clever, otherwise he wouldn't have gotten caught so damn easily. So that brings us to another lead, 'God.'

"Repeatedly Gary said God told him 'X' and God told him 'Y.' What if this 'God' does exist, what if this 'God' was communicating with Gary somehow, planting ideas in his head, giving him tip-offs, radicalizing Gary without leaving any evidence of his existence?

"We think 'God' is an alias for some kind of computer hacker. An individual with counterintelligence skills, able to access confidential information, contact targets then vanish, covering their tracks. They could be ex-Russian Intelligence, North Korean, hell even ex-MI5. Or just some geek in their mum's attic. Point is, this is the modern world and individuals with these skills *do exist*. 'God' could be a new breed of cyber terrorist, who brainwashes and activates easily manipulated loners to carry out these crimes.

"What if Gary is just a pawn in a much larger endgame? What if 'God' is contacting and activating more 'Gary's' as we speak? We need to know. That is why we have been given the go-ahead to set up a new taskforce, a long-term investigation unit that will run parallel to regular operations. This new taskforce is code named G.H.U: the God Hunter Unit.

"The aim is to track cyber chatter. We'll be examining cold cases, following up on any loose ends and leads pertaining to this case and others like it. So, enjoy tonight, take a few days off this weekend, see the family, have a beer, and take a rest. You'll need it, because as of next Monday G.H.U is active, and we'll be hunting God!"

SOMEWHERE
IN HEAVEN

God, shape shifting through identities, looked out over it's shape shifting orchard, musing on the recent events.

"What's the status, Gov?" asked the assistant.

"I had to let him go," answered God with a resigned tone.

"That's a pity, Gov."

"A pity indeed. Tell me, when did we lose control of the courts?"

"That was the 10th century, Gov."

"Huh, feels like yesterday. But oh well. We know this targeted method works, now we just need the numbers."

"How's that going, Gov?"

"Reasonable. We have about one hundred prophets of death in the initial stages of development in the UK alone. Of that number at least three are already learning to make 'The Gift.' I'm building a network of them this time. They're to communicate anonymously over their 'internet'. That way they can be self-organized, have strength in numbers, start recruiting, grow organically and spread the message. Plus, I've given them the full 'kill list' this time. It contains names, faces and locations of all the earth souls to be fast tracked to Heaven, so now I won't have to do nearly as much hand holding, they're free to just get on with it."

"Good idea, Gov.' Much harder to stop than lone operators."

"Exactly, Gary's takedown taught us something at least."

"How big is the kill list now, Gov?"

"About 15 million in the UK," grinned God, winking with its infinite eyes.

From the shadows of the room, Julie watched the shifting identities that is God, talking to itself. Julie's Human-Angel part of her soul perceived the shifting being subjectively as a twenty-foot-tall super woman, glowing with bright white light, its physique a combination of marbled beauty and impossible strength, an undefeatable foe. Yet Julie's Demon part of her soul perceived the entity as nothing more than a worm, emanating a dull white glow, wriggling on a golden tiled floor.

She embraced her Demon side and emerged from the darkness. She plucked the worm from the ground and held it between her fingers, dangling it in front of her Demon-Angel-human eyes, watching the dim glow of sublime power shine from within its translucent, squirming body.

"Time for change" she thought, then dropped the Holy Worm into her mouth and swallowed.

CHAPTER 12

Carrying the welcome bag of supplies, the warden led Gary to the door.

He gave it a knock and slid open the hatch.

"You got a new roomy Keith, we're coming in."

The warden opened the cell door and beckoned Gary inside.

"In you go."

Gary gazed numbly around the box room, his bunk, then to his roommate Keith.

"How do you do?" said Gary politely, remembering his manners.

"Whatever, man," said Keith, giving him a funny look.

The warden closed the door behind him.

"Enjoy, fellas."

Gary sat on his bed and stared at the grimy, pen-graffitied wall. His face sagged as he disconnected from the world.

He could no longer feel God's presence. He wondered how God could just abandon him like this after everything he had done for him. A whole life spent in worship, prayer, devotion, and sacrifice.

Perhaps this was his final sacrifice, barred from any form of afterlife, good or bad.

He could not help muse on the contradiction that laid out before him; he'd been given holy freedom and thus released from the shackles of spiritual consequence, to live out the rest of his mortal life as he pleases without persecution. Yet his physical, mortal freedom has been taken from him, forever.

He laughed at the thought. He was free, but only free to live in a cage.

He applauded God's sense of humor. The divine irony. God exists, but just not for him.

Then a new feeling emerged. A feeling of dread. Dread that he was truly alone. Accountable for his own actions. He became aware of infinity and the void. No more God, no Satan, no Afterlife. Just this little insignificant life in a universe of black space and spinning rocks. He was at the helm of his own destiny and for the first time felt completely lost.

What does one do with nothing but time, with no

God to guide, no rule to follow?

Then he remembered the prison warden's instructions:

- **Lockdown:** between 6PM and 8AM.
- **Breakfast:** 8:30AM.
- **Lunch:** 12:00PM.
- **Dinner:** 5:00PM.
- **Recreation:** 1 hour in the yard.

He felt relief. Through the disorientation of endless possibility now emerged a structure. He would not have to think or make his own choices, for in prison those choices were made for him. What to do and when to do it. At that moment, the void shrank. It no longer seemed relevant. He concluded that this was the best place for him to be. True freedom terrified him to the point where he would rather have no freedom at all.

"Oi, mush! Are you in there or what?" Keith said, waving his hand in front of Gary's eyes.

Gary snapped out of his thought cycle and acknowledged his cellmate.

"Oh, I'm sorry, hello," he said, trying to act normal.

"Mush, you was miles away, I've been chatting at you for the last two minutes."

"I apologise, I guess this is all a bit overwhelming for me."

"That's alright, mush. What's it like your first time inside or summin?"

"Yes, yes, it is. How about you?"

"Ah nah mush, I've been commin' here, in and out for time, y'nah what I mean, like since I was a nipper."

"What for?"

"All sorts, mate. Drug dealing, feevin cars, GBH, gang shit, you know, this and that. Anyways I didn't catch your name, mush?"

"Sorry, my names Gary, Gary Uxbridge."

"Gary Uxbridge…" Keith chewed on the name for a bit, then, after a few seconds he waved a knowing finger at Gary and smiled.

"Yeah, I fought I knew who you was, yeah."

"Sorry have we met before?"

Keith laughed.

"Ha, fuck no, I don't fink we'd have crossed paths mush. Different sides of the tracks, no what I mean, nah, you was on the news mush, that's why I knew your face, you're famous."

"Famous?" Gary was taken aback. He had no idea he had made the news.

"Yeah mush, you're that attempted serial killer int'ya. Us boys been creasing up at you trying all that 'God told me to do it' bullshit, tryin' to pretend you're crazy. Classic. Didn't work though, did it?"

"Apparently not," Gary said, smiling along with Keith. He had no reason to explain *it was* in-fact God's plan, not now he was forsaken.

"Yeah, but it nearly worked though didn't it, cos you're like a catholic priest or summin', yeah? So, they could have believed you, right?"

"I wasn't a Catholic Priest."

"Nah mush, you was, don't lie," Keith said smiling, waiving his finger at Gary again.

Gary laughed along.

"I was a vicar for the Church of England, not a Roman Catholic."

"Oh, sorry mush. My mistake. Still, it's kinda the same fing, innit? You know, vicar, priest, churches, God shit. Know what I mean?"

"Yeah, I suppose it is all the same really," Gary smiled and raised his eyebrows in agreement.

"Haha told ya mush. Yeah, they're the same. Part from catholic priests like to fuck kids," Keith said, laughing.

Keith stopped laughing and glared at Gary with an accusing eye.

"Do you like to fuck kids, Gary?" he asked.

"What? No, of course not, I would never do that," Gary exclaimed feeling unfairly accused.

"But you just said you and catholic priests are the same fing, like two seconds ago. So, if catholic priests are paedo's, then you're a paedo, innit."

"Whoa, whoa, that's not what I meant. We are not like that. I'm not like that."

"You calling me thick mush? You lying to me, saying one fing then another? You takin' the piss outa me?"

"I would never call you thick. I'm not lying to you. Sorry if I've offended you. I'm sorry, I don't know what is happening. I thought we were just talking?"

Gary felt a palpable danger in the room now.

There was a long pause as Keith stared at him with intense accusing eyes. He then burst into laughter.

"Ah I'm just playing wiv-ya mush, I'm just playin', I believe ya," Keith said, waving his hands.

"Wow, few. You really had me going there," Gary said, laughing with relief.

Keith laughed some more and then put his hands back down to his sides and smiled. Making eye contact once again.

"But it is true, right, that the prosecution got some shrink to say you had sexual feelings about kids, and that's why you killed that woman and wanted to kill that man. Cos you was 'projecting' or summin?"

"That did happen, yes. But they only said that to use as a motive against me. But it's not true at all."

"Yeah, but it's on your record, innit?"

"It is on the record. But it's not true. I've never had feelings towards kids or anything like that."

"Don't worry mate, I believe you, you don't need to convince me, I can tell you ain't lying."

"Good."

"But you gotta admit, it doesn't look good, does it, you being a priest, sorry, vicar, and that being on you're record. That word being on the street, you know?"

"Yeah, I suppose you're right."

"And the thing is mush, is that everyone in here has seen your papers. All them boys on the block, they fink you're a fucking nonce."

"OK... What does that mean, how do I convince them otherwise, do I need to watch my back, can you talk to them for me?"

"Well, mush, I'll tell ya now. The two things you don't want to get labeled as, is a grass or a nonce."

"What happens if you get that label?"

Keith moved his eyes menacingly around the cell, insinuating the prison as a whole.

"The rule is in here, grasses and nonces gotta get fucked up."

"Oh, wow. I'll watch out then. Thanks," Gary said, looking around the cell, feeling worried.

"And, well, the other rule is, if someone doesn't hit that nonce or grass when they could have, then people will fink that they must be a grass or a nonce too. Then they gotta get fucked up as well."

"Well thanks for letting me know Keith. What should I do now? I don't want any trouble with anyone," Gary said, imagining the rooms and rooms of inmates wanting to have a go at him.

"Sorry mush, you can't do nuffin."

Gary then felt three blunt impacts to the side of his neck.

"Ow! what the...?"

Disorientated he looked across at Keith, who was still sitting in the same place he sat before Gary had looked away, yet now he appeared flustered and pumped up, still staring at Gary.

Gary followed the spatter of blood on Keith's face down to the inmates' right hand, which held what seemed to be a sharpened toothbrush handle.

Gary began to notice a sensation on his left shoulder, streams of liquid, soaking through the fabric of his shirt.

He put his hand to his neck. It was wet and warm. Confused, he inspected his hand, only to find it was covered in thick, bright red blood. His blood.

Then he realised what had happened.

Pain and fear kicked in as Gary fell back on his bunk, his hand back on his neck, putting pressure on the stab wounds.

He began to wail and scream and gargle as blood sprayed through his fingertips.

"Oh god, oh god. No, no, help, somebody help me. Please, God, please help me!"

Gary heard his cries emanating from himself, as he stared at the ceiling.

But there was no voice of God, no divine presence. Just the noise of his own mind, ringing like a fire alarm over the sound of his gargled screams.

He could feel his life-force dimming, the noise getting duller.

He realised this is what Julie McBride must have felt, the fear, the loneliness. He felt regret. But she was in Heaven. A place he could never be. He knew that now.

He watched as the cell door swung open and a guard tackled Keith to the ground. There was shouting and swearing and commotion.

His vision was dimming.

He saw a second guard standing over him. Placing a hand to his neck, blood spraying onto the guard's face like a tap.

"You're alright mate, you're alright. Someone get a fucking doctor!"

Gary could hear the voice above the ringing in his head.

Seconds passed like minutes.

Gary could only see darkness now. The black inside his own head.

The voices began to fade until he could hear only the static of his own mind.

A white noise.

He thought about the unfairness of it all...

...and

...finally

...there

...was

...silence.

SOMEWHERE IN HEAVEN

Julie McBride sat on the beach with white sands and a shimmering white sea. The white sun warmed her face as she watched the tide that made no sound. Just silence, tranquil, blissful, silence.

No human soul, nor no Angel could bother her now. This was her beach, her Heaven. She had ascended.

"How would you like to handle PR, ma'am?" asked the assistant.

"Tell them God is dead; Heaven is under new management now. There's going to be some changes around here," instructed Julie.

"Very good, ma'am. I'll update the press release."

"Thank you," Julie wiggled her toes in the white sand and turned her attention back to the tide, "anything else?"

"Yes, sorry ma'am. I think I should warn you that once word gets out that God is dead, it could lead to a bit of instability and civil unrest around here. I mean, I can think of at least one person who might have a problem with you being in charge."

"Let me guess, that psycho, Jesus."

"He is, technically, the rightful heir to the throne, ma'am, and he does have the people on his side. He could lead an uprising against you."

"OK, I want him banished or imprisoned and I want it done now. Afterall, without his influence maybe Heaven won't be such a disgusting blood bath, he's always whipping the souls up into a frenzy."

"Very good, ma'am, he does bring out the worst in people."

"Thank you, is there anything else?"

"Yes, ever so sorry ma'am, you should be aware that the news of God's demise will eventually reach Hell, and when it does, you can be sure Lucifer will want to make a move on Heaven."

"Make a move, you mean invade?"

"Yes, ma'am."

"So, you're telling me not only do I have to watch my back with my own people, but I also have to worry about a full-scale invasion from the armies of Hell?"

"Ever so sorry ma'am, God had a peace treaty with Hell; each party agreed to put down their weapons and stick to their own domains, then compete for souls on earth rather than war against each other. But I can't imagine Lucifer of all people honoring that arrangement now."

"What defenses do we have?"

"Well, you've got an army of Angels, ma'am. But a lot of them will be loyal to Jesus."

"OK, how about this, can we use our supply of human souls as a first wave shield against the armies of Hell, at least until we get the Angels on side."

"Souls as cannon fodder, very good, ma'am. I'll start making arrangements."

"Thank you," Julie sat back in the sand and watched the waves, content things were being handled.

She was alone.

She was content.

Deep within her bowels shone a light in the darkness, a luminescent worm wriggled.

"Mayday! Mayday! Is anybody out there, I repeat, is anybody out there?"

"We're in a bit of pickle, aren't we, Gov?"

"To bloody right we are. We're being slowly digested

in the guts of a hybrid megalomaniac, and I can't get a signal out to anyone on Heaven or Earth."

"Have you tried Nowhere, Gov?"

"Uh, no…Satan and I agreed that place was off limits. If I contact Nowhere, if I even can, then the peace treaty fails and war with Hell is inevitable."

"I think, considering the circumstances, it's worth a shot, Gov."

"OK, you're right. Let's see if this works. Mayday! Mayday! This is God. Can anybody hear me? I repeat this is God, this is an emergency, can anybody hear me, is anybody out there?"

"…Hello?"

"Hi, yes great, I know this might sound strange, but I am God and I'm in a bit of a palaver. I could do with some assistance. To whom am I speaking with?"

"…Is, is that really you, My Lord? Have you come back to me, am I no longer forsaken, Father?"

"Holy shit! Gary, is that you?"

SPECIAL THANKS

Charlotte Hunter,
Simon Gardiner,
Andy Reville,
Charlotte Van Wijk,
John Ash,
Mike White,
Claire Shackleton,
Spencer Marshman,
Bertille Bacart,
Chris Robinson,
Abbie and Dave,
Roisin Kay,
Tom and Sheila,
Mum and Dad,
Grandad.

ABOUT THE AUTHOR

Matt

Is a British author based in Hampshire, Southern England.

His debut book is the novella GOD'S GIFT, first published in Oct 2021.

Aside from writing, Matt has a professional background in Data Analytics, and is also a practicing visual artist with a degree in contemporary fine art (which he never fails to mention.)

In his spare time he eats pasta, tinkers on the guitar, watches tonnes of movies, plays PC games badly, and battles a serious YouTube addiction.

Printed in Great Britain
by Amazon